The Cinderella Scheme

Toni Blake

Dear Reader,

This is one of three books published at the beginning of my career under the pen name Toni Blair. Unfortunately, when they first released in the late 90s, the length limitations of the publisher required these novels to be shortened by approximately one-third of their original length, altering my vision for the stories significantly. So I'm pleased to be able to present, for the first time anywhere, the full and extended versions of these books.

As I read over my original manuscripts and polished up the words a little, I realized that I could not write these same books now—I discovered in them a certain youthfulness and innocence that came from just that, my youth, and my more limited worldview at the time. I'm a very different person and writer than I was then, and it was both enlightening and invigorating to revisit these stories, getting reacquainted with my younger writing self and seeing parts of myself I'd long since forgotten. As part of preserving the context of that worldview, I've chosen to keep this book in its original 1996 setting, not updating for technology or other lifestyle changes.

It is with great joy that I present to you *The Cinderella Scheme* as I intended it to be read. I hope you will enjoy it!

Toni Blake

Chapter One

L OOKING INTO THE tiny mirror in the break room of
Fast Eddie's Diner, Cassie Turner swept her hair up
off her neck and into a pink ponytail holder. She hated
its color—a dreary shade of dishwater blond. She grimaced at her reflection and ran her fingers through her
thin bangs, trying to make them do something—
anything—but they merely lay on her forehead looking
flat and dull. "Dumb hair," she muttered toward the
mirror.

"What'd you say?" her friend and fellow waitress
Jewel asked, approaching from behind. Large earrings
dangled nearly to Jewel's shoulders, their red and purple
beads clashing with her pink uniform.

"Nothing," Cassie replied. "Just wishing…" *for a better job, a better life, a better future.* It was 1996, she was
twenty-five years old, and she couldn't shake the feeling
that life was passing her by. The noise of the "L" rum-
bling past outside the diner blotted out the sound of her
sigh. "Just wishing for better hair," she finally said, still
peering helplessly into the glass.

Jewel shook her head, obviously annoyed. "You've got great hair, Cassie. You just need to floof it up some."

"Floof it up?"

Jewel attended hair design school at night, but her terminology often came out sounding less than technical. Now she raked her fingers through her own voluminous dark hair in a manner that suggested lifting and fluffing. "Like this," she explained. "I could do it for you—"

"No, you couldn't," Cassie cut her off. Jewel's taste was a bit wild, and despite repeated promises of conservatism, Cassie wasn't sure she could trust her friend.

"Hey Cass, you working today or just playing beauty shop?" their boss Eddie thundered, cutting through the conversation. "Got a table of big spenders out here and nobody to take their order."

Jewel always claimed that Eddie's bark was worse than his bite, but Cassie jerked to attention anyway. "Coming, Eddie," she said, rushing through the grease-laden kitchen, then grabbing a handful of white laminated menus. A glance into the dining area revealed four suits in a booth near the door, so she hurriedly filled four small water glasses, placed them on a tray, and moved toward her customers.

"Sorry to keep you waiting." She briskly placed the glasses on the table, one by one.

"No problem," replied the smoothest, deepest voice she'd ever heard.

Her eyes subtly made their way toward the voice as she distributed the plastic menus. The suit who had spoken had dark brown hair, cut short in back, but a few wayward locks fell down over his forehead, suggesting that there was more than a professional side to his personality. To call him handsome would have been a gross understatement. *Overwhelmingly, devastatingly* handsome was more like it. His alluring smile made Cassie's chest tighten with quick desire as his green eyes pinned her in place. And as for his companions, they could have been aliens—Cassie didn't even notice them.

Was this love? Lust? Cassie couldn't tell the difference at the moment, and she only prayed her reaction didn't show on her face. She licked her lips quickly, realizing they'd gone suddenly dry, then attempted to speak. "What would you like?" Though her eyes stayed glued to the object of her desire. So much for subtlety.

"The specials, Cassie!" Eddie bellowed though the window behind the counter. "Tell them the specials."

"Oh yeah," she muttered, glancing briefly over her shoulder. Eddie's booming voice had shaken her from her trance—both a relief and a disappointment. Turning back to the table, she deliberately fixed her gaze on the napkin holder in the center. That would be much safer than mooning at the man with the fabulous eyes. And it was her only hope of getting through this with any dignity.

"We have a chicken and dumpling plate with two side items for $5.99 and a pork barbecue sandwich with cole slaw and baked beans for $6.99. Are you ready to order or do you need a few minutes?"

That was when Cassie accidentally lifted her gaze to Mr. Green Eyes, having already forgotten the effect it would have on her. And oh God—he was looking back. Her heart beat wildly and she knew all attempts at dignity were futile.

"I think I'll try the barbecue." He flashed another smile. "And a glass of iced tea."

Cassie swallowed. "Great," she mumbled as she scribbled furiously on her order pad. Unbeknownst to him, it was more an observation about the way he looked than a response to his order.

She gripped her pen tightly, palms now sweating, as the other three men placed their orders as well. But oh brother—her concentration had completely evaporated; she had to repeat two of the orders back to make sure they were correct.

After finally getting them right, she made a beeline for Eddie. "Here," she said, shoving the orders into his waiting fist. Then she rushed breathlessly to Jewel, who sat reading a fashion magazine in the break room. "Help me," she pleaded.

"Help you what?"

"There's, there's…" she could hardly talk. "There's a gorgeous man in our dining room and I, I…"

"Want me to do your hair?" Jewel suggested hopefully.

Cassie shook her head frantically, ponytail swinging behind. "No. I need a pep talk. Some advice. What to say. How to act. Anything."

Jewel looked introspective. "What are you trying to get out of this? A good tip, a roll in the hay—what?"

Cassie's heartbeat slowed when she realized that she had no idea *what* she really wanted. And that this was a response she'd never had to a customer before. After all, she waited on lots of men here every day, but never before had one had this effect on her. There had simply been something about him, about the moment, that she'd felt compelled to grab on to, to not let pass her by. Even if she couldn't really explain to herself—or anyone else apparently—why. "Just...to make a good impression," she finally said, for lack of a better answer.

Jewel rose from the table and skirted quickly past Cassie to poke her head around the corner where she could spy on the customers. "Let me guess," she said. "Tall, dark, and hot, next to the window."

Cassie nodded.

"Afraid I'm the wrong person to ask about hobnobbing with a suit-and-tie guy, Cass," Jewel told her matter-of-factly. "I'm more into the black leather type myself. All I can do is slap a little makeup on your face and possibly floof up your bangs some."

Cassie took a deep breath, considering the offer. "Okay, I'll take it." Even the vague *floofing* seemed better than nothing at the moment.

Jewel had just reached up toward Cassie's bangs when Eddie's voice broke through their conversation again. "Cassie?"

"What now?" Didn't he know she was in the middle

of a stressful situation?

Eddie leaned his balding head into the room. "Drinks," he said quietly. "Silverware." He seemed to be trying to new method of reasoning. "The gentlemen at table three need these things. It's the part of the job that comes between taking their orders and serving their food."

Cassie cautiously raised her eyes. "Sorry, Eddie," she said. "I'm having a weird day."

"I noticed," he muttered, withdrawing back to the kitchen.

"Guess your bangs are on their own," Jewel said. Then she playfully punched Cassie in the arm. "Knock 'em dead, kid."

Cassie moved swiftly behind the counter, her back to the four men as she assembled their drinks. At first she wondered if her green-eyed hunk might be watching her, studying her, and her heartbeat quickened with nervous anticipation.

But then reality set in. Why would a gorgeous guy like that look twice at a skinny, dowdy, pink-uniformed waitress like her? She was used to being ogled by the construction guys who came in for lunch, and she knew that Hank, the shy, overweight man who delivered their dairy products, had a crush on her. But Mr. Green Eyes was in a different league altogether.

Wait—what was she thinking? He was in a different galaxy.

Cassie had forced herself into a state of calm by the

time she moved back toward the table bearing drinks and silverware rolled in white napkins. This was just another table, after all. Another set of customers. One of them was extremely pleasant to look at, sure, but other than that, this was just another tip. *If* she could start acting a little more courteous and efficient, that was.

She lowered two cups of coffee in front of the men across from Mr. Green Eyes. Then she placed a soda before the man to his right.

She tried not to look at him. She really did. But there he was, his gaze shining up at her like she was the most important thing in the room, and she felt herself begin to tremble. Lord, what was happening here?

That's just how hot he is. So hot he makes you tremble. Never in her life had she suffered such an intense visceral reaction to a stranger.

Taking a deep breath and trying to shore up her nerves, she pulled her eyes away from him and back to the glass of iced tea that remained on her tray. She bit her lip as she carefully picked it up and leaned toward him over the table. And just as she began to wonder if he was able to see down the top of her uniform, the moisture on the outside of the plastic glass made her lose her grip.

The glass seemed to drop from her hand in slow motion, giving her time to think *why me?*, pray a helpless prayer, and lunge madly for the glass with her other hand, letting the tray clatter to the floor behind her. Despite all that, the glass clunked unevenly on the table, falling on its side and spewing its contents all over her gorgeous customer.

"Oh my God!" she gasped.

Mr. Green Eyes' companion moved quickly from the booth to let his wet friend stand. Cassie clenched her teeth in horror at the sight of the handsome, well-dressed man she'd just drenched in iced tea. This couldn't be happening. It just couldn't. She began shaking her head desperately. "I'm so, so sorry!" she spewed up at him.

Mr. Green Eyes brushed the excess wetness from his shirt and jacket lapels as she watched in dread. Finally it occurred to her to dash to the counter and grab a dry rag. She returned, still mortified, to begin blotting at the man's shirt and tie, trying to somehow fix what she'd done—although, like saving her dignity, this effort was just as useless.

"I can't believe I did that to you," she blurted in a rush, still blotting at him, and at the same time taking in the scent of musk that seemed to emanate from his body. "Your shirt," she went on, "and your suit." His clothes looked expensive—GQ all the way. "How can I…what can I…I'm so sorry!"

Only then did she notice that he was smiling down at her, his eyes nearly glittering beneath the fluorescent lighting. "No harm done," he said. "It's all dry-cleanable."

Oh wow, he was being so nice. But Cassie still couldn't believe what she'd done to him. Her eyes landed on his tie, obviously silk and obviously costly, now stained and soggy-looking. Without thinking, she reached out and touched it. With her fingertips lightly pressed to his chest, she bit her lip and peered up at him. "Even the tie?"

His eyes filled with sympathy, which wasn't exactly what she wanted from him, but it was better than anger or the host of other emotions that he *could* be displaying. His deep voice came out softer than before. "Well, the tie's probably shot," he admitted, "but it's no big deal."

She sighed heavily. How unbelievably awful and embarrassing—she'd ruined the perfect man's tie. "I'm so very sorry." Only then did she realize that she was practically petting the soggy silk tie now, and by association, the chest beneath it, as well. She let her hand drop abruptly and took a step back from him.

But he still smiled down at her. "The tie's not a big thing," he reassured her. "Really. Promise." And then he even winked. Which caused an unexpected twinge right between her legs. Oh my.

She let out another sigh, distraught now in more ways than she could even count. She couldn't believe she was such a klutz. With the most attractive man ever to cross her path. And that even in the midst of her klutziness, ribbons of arousal wove and twisted all through her. "I'm so, so sorry," she said again.

"It's all right. Truly," he insisted. "Probably your first day on the job or something, huh?"

Cassie peered up at him, blinking nervously. She'd been working at Fast Eddie's for almost six months.

"Yeah," she said, swallowing.

He nodded in understanding. "Don't sweat it," he told her, his tone that of a consoling camp counselor. "Things are bound to get better."

"Couldn't get much worse," she mumbled.

Then, still affecting his counselor attitude, he gently lifted her chin with one bent finger, the simple touch sending electric sensations soaring through her body from head to toe. "Look," he said softly, those green eyes boring into her, "this is nothing to get upset about. And I'd feel terrible if I thought I'd ruined your first day on a new job. So it's forgotten. Okay?"

Had she ever seen eyes any more sincere? She had no choice but to accept his forgiveness. "Okay."

"Order up," Eddie called through the window, plunking his palm down on the tiny bell on the ledge.

"Your food," she said to Mr. Green Eyes, pulling reluctantly away from his touch. "I'll try not to dump it on you," she promised as she started toward the counter.

With moves as delicate and painstaking as if she were building a house of cards, Cassie delivered each man's lunch, lowering the plates to the table with great care. She breathed a huge sigh of relief when the task was completed without mishap. She just hoped he hadn't noticed that her hands were quivering—a leftover reaction from his touch. "Will there be anything else right now?"

Mr. Green Eyes lifted his gaze and spoke softly. "Could I, um, get another glass of iced tea?"

CASSIE LEANED ABSENTLY against the counter and reached into the pocket of her apron to pull out the twenty-dollar bill and look at it again. She smoothed it between her fingers, still unable to believe it. The other men in the party had left the customary fifteen percent in singles and change scattered about the table, but the twenty had been tucked deliberately beneath the tall plastic tea glass.

Of course, a big tip was hardly an expression of love. And the tip certainly wasn't indicative of the fine service she'd given the man. It obviously meant that he'd felt sorry for her.

Still, it was an incredibly kind gesture to make toward someone who had spilled a drink on him and ruined an expensive tie. What a truly nice guy he must be.

A thick sense of infatuation pulsed through her every limb. Would he come in the diner again soon? Well, if he did, she'd certainly have to find some way to control her clumsiness.

As Eddie's paunchy form moved past her, he shook his head in disbelief. "Beats the hell out of me how you can make a mess of a guy's lunch and get twenty bucks out of it."

She shrugged her shoulders in agreement.

Her boss stopped then, tilting his head sideways. "What's going on with you today, anyway?"

"I don't know, Eddie, it's just..." *That I'm feeling plain and unattractive? Helpless and alone in a huge city? That I'm afraid this is as good as life gets—that the best, if there ever* was *any best, is all behind me now?* But Eddie wouldn't understand any of that. "Just having a weird day is all."

She thrust the twenty back into her apron and picked up a wet rag. She wiped down the counter, then started filling ketchup bottles to kill time before her shift ended. But soon she found herself stopping to stare out the large plate glass window at a businesswoman striding past on the sidewalk. The woman's tailored suit exuded authority without making her appear cold or bossy. Her hair was pulled back from her face in a way that looked both professional and elegant. Cassie sighed. Why couldn't that be her?

She'd left her small hometown of Hargrove, Kentucky just over six months ago and come to Chicago seeking…a life. Of some kind. She hadn't wanted to be a poor farmer like her father. Or a poor farmer's wife, no matter how many times Jimmy Hickson had asked her to marry him. She hadn't ever really loved Jimmy, and even if she had, she wasn't sure that was a good enough reason to give up her dreams. Besides, that had been a high school romance, over ages ago in her heart, and dragging on for far too long in reality.

At twenty-five, Cassie had finally faced the truth. She was an adult now. And she'd begun to feel like life was passing her by. If she wanted a real job, or a real chance at any kind of a fulfilling existence, she knew she had to leave her country community while leaving still felt like a viable option.

So she'd packed her bags and headed to the city, ready to attempt building a real life of her own.

She hadn't built much so far, though. Her job barely paid the bills. And she'd made only two real friends, Jewel and Mac—who, she realized as she checked her watch, would soon be waiting outside for her.

Sophisticated businesswomen often caught Cassie's eyes out the diner's big plate glass windows or in the booths she waited on, making her wish she could be like them. She longed to experience the purpose she saw in the way they walked, the sense of accomplishment that gleamed in their eyes. The thought usually inspired and depressed her all at once.

Today, though, as she refocused her attention on the ketchup bottles, her emotion leaned closer to depression. She knew that the woman who had just strode past was the kind of woman Mr. Green Eyes would want. In fact, for all she knew, that woman might be on her way to meet him right now. "Some silly waitress spilled iced tea all over me, dear," he might say laughingly when she commented on his appearance. And then they'd go home to some plush penthouse apartment and make love all night long.

She sucked in her breath at the pang of disappointment that struck with the thought of Mr. Green Eyes loving someone, anyone, who wasn't her.

Oh brother—talk about silly. What a ridiculous way to feel. She didn't even know the man!

But that didn't mean she didn't feel it. He was just so perfect—handsome, kind, confident, and beyond sexy. Or at least he certainly *seemed* like he'd be all those things.

As the "L" roared past outside just then, though, it shook her from her reverie. *Crushes on strangers are for little girls. Snap out of it. And you'll never see him again anyway.*

She recapped the ketchup bottles and returned them to the tables just as her shift ended at four. Time to meet Mac.

Leaning around the corner into the kitchen, she checked to make sure it was empty, which meant Eddie was taking his afternoon break, which—on a pretty day like this one—usually included a slow walk around the block. Then, moving to the work station where he made sandwiches, she quickly and quietly grabbed a loaf of bread and pulled out two slices. She slapped on some mustard with a knife, then reached in the deli case for some pre-sliced turkey and American cheese. When the sandwich was complete, she looked around for side items, deciding on cole slaw and baked beans, thinking of the meal she'd served Mr. Green Eyes earlier. Sloshing a large spoonful of each into small Styrofoam cups, she topped them with plastic lids and, lastly, grabbed up a fork. Then, balancing the small tower of food, she casually sauntered out the back door and into the grungy alley.

"Pssst," she said. "Mac, where are you?"

A small man wearing dirty clothes ambled from behind the Dumpster. He was old enough to be her grandfather. "Hi Cassie," he said, offering a small, almost toothless grin.

"Hey Mac." She returned the smile.

"What smells so good?"

"Probably the beans," she answered as he took the fork from her fingers and lifted the turkey sandwich from atop of the stack of food.

She watched as Mac wolfed down the sandwich in only a few bites. "Here." She offered him one of the Styrofoam containers. "Eat the beans before they get cold."

He smiled his appreciation as he took the white cup from her hand.

She'd found Mac hiding behind the diner one afternoon shortly after she'd started working at Eddie's—he'd been waiting for the garbage to be taken out. He'd been afraid of her at first, until he'd realized that she wasn't angry at him, or repulsed by him, and that she wasn't going to report him to Eddie or the police.

She knew what it was like to be poor, after all. She didn't know what it was like to be as poor as Mac, but who knew when she might find out? Her family had never been well off and she'd been living from paycheck to paycheck ever since coming to the city. She knew that for herself, and many people, homelessness could be a heartbeat away.

Each day when her shift ended, Cassie met Mac at the Dumpster. Knowing he got at least one decent meal five days a week helped her sleep better at night.

"Although I don't necessarily like you stealing," he'd once said to her.

"Well, it's not stealing exactly," she'd replied. "Eddie just made too much, that's all."

"Eddie makes too much every day?"

"So he's a bad judge of volume," she'd claimed. "That's no reason for it to go to waste."

She focused her thoughts back on the present. "Did you spend last night at the shelter?" she asked as he nearly sucked down the spicy baked beans.

He nodded, but looked forlorn. Mac didn't like the shelter, yet Cassie felt better when she knew he wasn't on the streets. "Some guy keeps bothering me while I try to sleep," he told her. "Some crazy guy."

She sighed. It was hard to know how to deal with the everyday terrors that made up Mac's life. "Still, it's safer than being outside," she told him. "Ask one of the workers to keep an eye on him. And I'll check on him myself on Saturday." She served lunch at the Sunshine House on weekends.

"That sandwich was tasty, Cassie, but tomorrow I sure could go for a piece of Eddie's chocolate cream pie."

She cast him a chiding look. "You know there's no nutritional value in that, Mac. If I'm going to be feeding you, I have to think about your health and stick to the good stuff."

He sighed in response. "All right," he said. "Let's not talk about me, then. How was your day?"

Despite herself, she fairly beamed. She hadn't planned on telling him about Mr. Green Eyes, but she couldn't contain herself. "I met a gorgeous man today, Mac."

He smiled back at her. "Sounds promising."

"It's not," she said matter-of-factly, coming back down to earth. "I dumped a glass of iced tea on him. But he was really wonderful. And handsome. And perfect."

Mac nodded.

"Rich, too," she added. "At least I think he was. Just the type of man I'll never have." She ended in a wistful sigh.

"I don't see why not," Mac said, taking the last course of his meal from her hand. "A pretty girl like you."

She met Mac's kind gaze, but then let her eyes drop to her gym shoes. "You're sweet, Mac, really. But this guy was way out of my league."

The old man grinned. "Gotta have faith, Cassie. Good things'll happen if you're patient and you believe."

"Believe in what?"

"Fate. Miracles."

She shook her head. Who believed in miracles anymore? "Come on, Mac, don't be silly. And besides, I'll never see him again."

Just then, the back door of the diner burst open and

Jewel came racing out. "Sorry to interrupt dinner, Mac," she said, "but Cassie, you're not gonna believe this!" She waved a newspaper in her fist.

"What?"

Jewel shoved the paper into Cassie's hands, then pointed directly at the man pictured there. "Look who it is, Cass. Your Prince Charming."

Chapter Two

CASSIE STARED AT the black-and-white picture on the front page of the business section as Jewel waited for her reaction. Oh God, it was him! She drew in her breath as she became reacquainted with his masculine perfection. Even in newspaper print—his vibrant green eyes demoted to gray—he was breathtaking.

The headline above the picture read *Princess Cosmetics Expands Kingdom*. She drew her gaze down to focus on the caption below the photo. *Evan Hunt, thirty and heir to the Princess Cosmetics throne, is solely responsible for the company's recent acquisitions. Hunt hopes that acquiring smaller companies will help Princess corner the market in this competitive industry.*

"Evan Hunt," she whispered. A handsome name for a handsome man. Her eyes rose back to his black-and-white face and she sighed with longing.

"So?" Jewel said, beaming at her.

"So what?"

"So, your man practically owns Princess Cosmetics! What do you think of *that?*"

"I can't afford them, so I've never used them."

Jewel let out a frustrated *huff.* "Not what do you think about the cosmetics, dummy. What do you think about *this?*" She pointed again at the picture in the paper. "About who he is?"

"Well," Cassie began, shoving the paper back toward her friend, "now I know exactly who I can't have." After all, any other response to this new knowledge would be totally impractical. If she'd thought he was in a different galaxy before, now the distance between them was utterly unfathomable.

Jewel grimaced. "Don't be so pessimistic."

Glancing back and forth between her two friends, it was obvious that Mac agreed with Jewel, but she thought they were both crazy. "*You guys,*" she said emphatically. "Wake up here. He's a business executive and heir to a corporate throne. I'm a waitress. He wears silk ties and Armani suits. I wear"—she looked down at her pink uniform dress—"this."

"So?" Jewel asked.

"So don't be ridiculous," Cassie said sensibly, shifting her weight from one foot to the other. And in fact, this was inspiring in her more sense than she'd shown on this topic all day. "The man was my customer today. I'll probably never see him again. And if I do, I'll probably just spill something on him. So let's just all forget about it and get on with our lives."

Silence filled the dank alley as Mac and Jewel both just stood there staring at her. Maybe she'd sounded gruff. But it just wasn't healthy to go around fantasizing about things that were totally out of the realm of possibility. Was it?

"I'm just saying," Jewel finally imparted, "that if you had to spill something on a guy, you picked a really good one to spill something on."

Mac stood behind Jewel, grinning knowingly, as Cassie rolled her eyes. They were both being silly. As silly as she'd been about Mr. Green Eyes earlier. And she, on the other hand, was going to do something very mature, and then she was going to let this whole matter drop.

She snatched the paper back from Jewel's hand. "I'm glad you found this, Jewel," she said, "because now I know where I can send him a new tie."

PRINCESS COSMETICS. THE words kept ringing in Cassie's ears. She'd seen ads for them on TV and in magazines all her life. She knew little about them except that their signature color was powder puff pink—which reminded her annoyingly of the uniform she still wore—and that they were way out of her price range.

Plodding up the city sidewalk with a warm June sun blasting down, she glanced down again at the picture of Evan Hunt on the newspaper she carried in her hand. Every time she looked at him, it set her heart spinning—and though she knew it probably wasn't healthy, she kept looking, again and again.

The blare of a horn jerked her eyes upward—she'd

nearly walked out in front of a car on Wacker Drive. Oops! She waved a useless apology at the angry driver, then finally rolled up the newspaper and shoved it into her purse, where Evan Hunt's beautiful face would be out of harm's way, and where it would hopefully keep *her* away from harm, as well.

It was a short walk to Marshall Field's, a place where she usually only window shopped. Today, though, she moved through the revolving door with purpose. Instantly overcome with all the sights and smells inside the large store, she decided to head straight to the men's department. She wasn't in the mood to punish herself by fawning over things she couldn't have—she'd done enough of that today already.

But she was stopped cold by the large pink Princess Cosmetics display that stood a foot taller than her next to a long glass counter. The display beckoned to her— although its pink hue was almost garish in a way—and she knew that, for her, the real appeal lay not in the cosmetics or the display itself, but in the man behind the business.

Pink tubes and jars and bottles, all parading the word *Princess* in thick script letters, filled the glass case next to the cardboard display. The culmination of all the pink was a bit overwhelming, yet seeing the word again and again—*Princess, Princess, Princess*—made her feel somehow envious. Of the women who could afford to wear this stuff? Or of the women who could afford Evan Hunt?

"Can I help you?"

She lifted her gaze to the matronly woman behind the counter who eyed her critically. Glancing down at her uniform and the worn gym shoes that completed the outfit, Cassie gently shook her head. "No," she whispered.

And this just proved how right she'd been to tell herself she could never have a man like Evan Hunt. Apparently she couldn't even look at his company's products without drawing unwanted attention to herself. She turned and moved away from all the pinkness, dead set on finding the men's department without further delay.

When she finally did, she spotted expensive ties lying on round, mahogany tables, cascading like large silk pinwheels. She approached them cautiously, searching for the tie Evan Hunt had worn today—mostly blue with tiny flecks of deep red and gold.

She had nearly given up on finding the correct tie— what were really the chances anyway?—when she spotted it peeking from beneath an electric purple one. She pulled it free of the pinwheel design to study it—and yes, this was definitely the same tie he'd been wearing.

She ran her hand down over its luxurious softness, quickly remembering how she had almost petted the man's chest. Everything inside her grew warm as the memory sent a rush of heat creeping up over her cheeks. Yet then she pushed the whole event to the back of her mind—she had business to conduct, after all, and no time for useless daydreaming.

She flipped over the tie's price tag—$52! Geez, she'd never have dreamed they even *made* ties that expensive. She'd planned to use her twenty-dollar tip on the tie, along with the rest of today's tip money, but she'd have to add more.

Could she really make herself spend that much money on a tie? Her stomach sank at the thought. God knew she couldn't afford to go tossing money around—$52 could pay her light bill for a couple of months—but she couldn't shake the need to replace what she'd ruined after Evan Hunt had been so terribly nice to her.

It was the right thing to do.

And the classy thing to do.

And she very much wanted to be classy. So she bought the tie.

EVAN HUNT FLIPPED off his computer and ran his hands back through his hair. His eyes ached. He was tired of looking at numbers that seemed not to change no matter how he moved them around, no matter how hard he tried to make financial repairs to his family's business. Every time he thought about the possibility of Princess Cosmetics' demise, it felt as if an anchor weighed down his chest.

It was useless to discuss it with his aging father, who had refused for years to see Princess's problems and now spent most of the year vacationing in Arizona. Fixing the problems that had been allowed to fester for nearly a decade since his mother's death was a task that fell completely on Evan's shoulders.

Tossing his jacket over his shoulder, he turned off the lamp on his desk and left his office. "Gone for the day," he told Miriam, his administrative assistant and sometimes mother hen, as he passed by her desk.

"Get some sleep, Evan," she told him. "You're going to get bags under your eyes and then the pretty girls won't give you a second look." Then she gave him the same wink she'd been giving him for twenty-five years— only it didn't come with a lollipop anymore. Miriam had been his mother's AA, too—though they'd called her a secretary in those days—and had been with the company since Evan was five years old.

He smiled at the familiar gesture, but responded, "Afraid pretty girls are the last thing on my mind these days, Miriam." Then he rushed for the elevator and stepped inside just as the door began to close.

Only Miriam and the board of directors were privy to Princess's financial woes. The press saw their recent acquisitions as bold steps for the future when they were actually desperate grabs at trying to save today. The sales just weren't there, and no one had ever been able to run this company besides his mother, the late Evelyn Hunt.

He shook his head as he stepped from the elevator into the building's pink marble lobby. Damn, he was sick of pink. Pink bottles and containers. Pink brochures. Even the sign in front of the building was that same sickening pink.

But just relax. Try to leave work at work for once. That was a tall order, but at least he had something to distract him tonight—the charity dinner dance for the city's homeless. At two hundred dollars a plate, he hardly thought it prudent that he'd bought up two entire tables in his company's name, but it had seemed like the right thing to do. At any rate, it might be fun to go out for a change rather than sitting at home mulling over his problems.

He was walking toward his parking garage when he decided to take a short detour. He'd left in plenty of time to prepare for the evening ahead, so he had a few minutes to run into Marshall Field's and pick up a new tie to replace the stained one he still wore.

Once inside the store, he headed for the men's department, cornering the first saleslady he spotted. He held up his tie. "I bought this here last week and spilled something on it today. Do you have any more like it?"

The elderly saleswoman clasped her hands consolingly. "I'm sorry, but I just sold the last one to a young lady not five minutes ago."

He shrugged. Like he'd told the waitress at lunch, it wasn't a big deal—he'd just thought he'd pop in and see if they had another one. "Thanks anyway."

"We have some other lovely ties by the same maker if you'd like to see them."

He shook his head and offered a small smile. "Thanks, but I'll pass for now."

As he pulled his car into rush hour traffic a few minutes later, he thought again of his lunch today and the cute waitress who had spilled an entire glass of tea on him. It had been impossible to be mad at her with those big, innocent blue eyes and that adorable pout on her lips. Then he remembered how she'd blushed when she'd realized she was stroking his tie. As a smile came over him, he couldn't help thinking it was nice to have something to smile about, even if it was only something little: a memory of a pretty girl with wide eyes.

CASSIE UNLOCKED THE large steel door that led to her apartment. Well, it wasn't an apartment exactly. It was more like a warehouse. Okay, it actually *was* a warehouse.

Jewel's cousin owned the building and had offered to rent part of it to her cheap until he found a new tenant. She dreaded when that day came. It was by far the least expensive place to be had in the city and she could barely make ends meet as it was. It was a dump, but it was roomy. And her secondhand furniture looked right at home.

She glanced down at the handful of mail she'd just retrieved from her mailbox—yuck, mostly bills. Stepping inside, she dropped them on her kitchen table and moved to the living area, trying to forget about them. Then she fell onto the couch, kicked off her old shoes, and plopped her tired feet on the scarred coffee table. It had been a long day.

Only then did she look down at the flat narrow box she still held in her hand after the long walk home. She opened it up and studied the tie inside. Then she reached down and touched it with her fingertips, savoring the feel of the silk.

Bad, bad, bad, she scolded herself, jerking her hand back and promptly closing the box. Because touching the tie meant more than just touching the tie and she knew it. It was more like an attempt to touch the man for whom the tie was intended. Touching something that would soon be wrapped around him somehow seemed almost as good. Still, it was a fruitless endeavor.

Tomorrow she would tape up the box and address it to Evan Hunt at Princess Cosmetics. Then she would take it to the post office and spend yet more money on postage. She wouldn't enclose a note, because she didn't want it to be viewed as a come-on. And also because she didn't want it to actually *be* a come-on, which any note she wrote would certainly be. She just wanted to replace the man's tie and be done with it. Life was challenging enough without inviting the heartbreak that was sure to follow if she started chasing a guy who could never want her.

When the phone rang, she groaned. She didn't want to answer it. She was too tired. And too comfortable in her spot on the old couch. But she didn't have an answering machine and always feared that if she didn't pick up, it would turn out to be something important like a family emergency or someone wanting to give her a million dollars. So she dragged her tired limbs up off the couch and over the cool concrete floor to the phone next to her bed. "Hello."

"Thank God you answered!"

Cassie sighed. "This better be good, Jewel. I just got in the door and I'm beat."

"Well, get un-beat and put on your dancing shoes!"

Cassie shook her head—what had gotten into Jewel? "I can't get un-beat, and I don't own any dancing shoes. What's going on?"

"You won't believe this."

"Well, try me. And make it quick. There's a pot pie in the freezer calling my name."

"Forget your pot pie, kid. You're eating high on the hog tonight. I just snagged us two tickets to the biggest, fanciest bash in town."

"Jewel, what are you talking about?"

"I walked into hair school and my teacher gave me two tickets to this big charity thing tonight. She got them from her neighbor, who got them from her boss, and they supposedly cost two hundred bucks apiece."

"Would you slow down? What kind of charity thing?"

"Some kind of a dinner dance. Expensive food and probably everyone who's ever been on the *Tribune*'s society page. Sound like a blast?"

Despite Jewel's enthusiasm, Cassie didn't really think so. "Jewel," she complained, "I'm really tired, and I have nothing to wear. And besides, doesn't that sound like someplace where we'd be terribly out of place?"

She could hear Jewel *tsk tsk*ing on the other end of the phone. "How will you ever be a big, fancy business-woman if you don't learn to fit in with people like this? And how could you possibly think of passing up a two-hundred-dollar meal?"

Jewel was right, she supposed. At least about the first part. Being easily intimidated would get her nowhere in this world. And remembering how she'd crumbled today in front of Evan Hunt only reaffirmed that belief. She did hope to make more of herself than a waitress—she could have been a waitress back in Hargrove, after all—even if she had no idea how she was going to do it. "Still, Jewel, you know neither one of us has anything to wear to that kind of shindig."

But when Jewel merely chuckled, Cassie supposed she should have realized she'd be on top of the situation. "Get this," she said. "You know my friend, Irma, who works at Marshall Field's? Well, she has the authority to lend out eveningwear to people like us who are going to fancy high-profile events."

"She does?" It sounded preposterous.

"Sure," her friend claimed. "They do it in Holly-wood all the time. They think maybe someone will see you in it and want to know where you got it. It's like advertising. So what do you say?"

Still Cassie hesitated. "I don't know. Sounds weird wearing dresses that aren't ours."

"Cassie," Jewel said, reasoning with her, "this is the chance of a lifetime. I'll come over and fix your hair—conservatively, I promise. Then we'll go pick out dresses, put on makeup, and have the night of our lives. What better do you have to do? And how often does a chance like this come along?"

CASSIE PEERED IN the mirror in the dressing room of Marshall Field's eveningwear department. She couldn't believe what she saw. Her blond hair had been swept into a delicate up-do with thin wisps of loose hair curving toward her face. A strapless dress of ivory molded to her body, stopping just above the knees, and coordinating heels with sparkly rhinestones near her toes completed the outfit. It was difficult to fathom that only a few hours ago she'd been slinging hash at Fast Eddie's Diner.

She couldn't help casting a small smile at her own reflection. She'd have never believed she could look so sophisticated. She'd purposely chosen the ivory dress in hopes of appearing a little bit sexy and completely classy. Her stomach swam with butterflies at knowing with full confidence that she'd accomplished both.

She glanced at Jewel, who stood before another nearby mirror, decked out in red sequins and five-inch heels. After watching Jewel paint a bold red mouth onto her face, she then turned her attention back to her own makeup. Digging a tube of creamy rose-colored lipstick from the matching purse that Irma had insisted on adding to the ensemble, she applied it softly to her lips while Irma argued with Jewel behind her, demanding that Jewel put on the sheer jacket that came with the red dress, suggesting that she could wear it at dinner, then shed it for the dancing portion of the evening. Jewel finally conceded, and Cassie felt strangely as if she and her friend were getting ready for the prom. She expected Irma to start snapping pictures at any second.

But getting ready for the prom hadn't been this exciting. The dress she'd worn to the prom had been a girlish, frumpy hand-me-down from her cousin, whereas the one she wore now was the height of class and elegance. She'd gone to the prom with boring Jimmy Hickson, and tonight her companion was the fun and much more unpredictable Jewel.

The prom had been a fixed equation. She'd known what to expect, what the evening would hold. And it had lived up to her mediocre expectations. But tonight was different. Tonight was a mystery. It was exciting. Alluring. And there was nothing mediocre about it.

Despite her earlier protests, her heart beat a little faster as she anticipated the evening ahead.

CASSIE BALANCED PRECARIOUSLY on her borrowed high heels as she scaled the plush winding staircase that led to the second floor banquet room. All around her, high society buzzed. Men in tuxedos escorted women wearing glittery dresses, and women's ears and necks dripped with diamonds. Crisply uniformed waiters circulated with silver trays containing hors d'oeuvres and glasses of wine. What on earth was she doing here? Despite having convinced herself that it might be a good chance to meet important people, she began to regret her enthusiasm.

Her original fear had come true. "We don't fit in here, Jewel," she leaned over to whisper as they reached the top of the stairs.

"Of course we don't," Jewel replied. "But we look like we do and that's the important thing. The rest can be faked."

"I'm no good at faking," Cassie complained.

Jewel simply shot her a look of disdain, and she knew it was too late to back out now, no matter how badly she wanted to.

"Look," Jewel said. "*That* should inspire you." Cassie followed Jewel's pointing finger to a sign that stood near the polished wooden doors of the banquet hall. It read *Third Annual Dinner to Aid the Homeless*.

She sighed—Jewel was right. Seeing the sign, and the reason for the event, helped ease Cassie's worries. It took her mind away from her own small problems and helped her focus on the bigger picture. She thought of Mac, so patiently waiting for something good to happen in his life, and decided that maybe those hopes weren't all in vain—maybe someone else cared, someone with enough money to make a difference.

Dinner consisted of prime rib, twice-baked potatoes,

and a variety of side dishes she didn't recognize. She had heard that the tastes of the well-to-do sometimes didn't mesh with average people like herself, but to her pleasant surprise, she found the entire meal delicious, right down to the rich chocolate truffle served for dessert.

Being seated at a table with eight strangers, all of whom were senior citizens of the wealthiest variety, made her even more nervous, but thanks to Jewel's quick thinking, all went well. When asked about their presence at the high society event, Jewel simply explained that they were visiting from out of town, here on business. And as if on cue, one of the event's organizers came over to thank them all for coming, squelching further small talk for the moment.

"Scrumptious," one of the older ladies remarked, laying down her spoon after the last bite of truffle.

Cassie agreed with a smile. Fitting in with these people wasn't so difficult, after all.

"What company did you ladies say you were doing business with?" the woman's husband then leaned around her to inquire. Uh-oh—back to that again. Cassie tried to keep her eyes from going wide as she kicked Jewel under the table.

"Princess," Jewel replied easily. "Princess Cosmetics."

Oh Lord. Princess? Of all the companies in the world, Jewel had chosen to say they were with Princess? Cassie involuntarily sucked in her breath and began to choke.

As Jewel casually passed her a water glass, she made an obvious attempt to twist the conversation away from the company itself. "We're staying in a suite in the Hyatt. Lovely accommodations."

The man guffawed. "Why, I'm surprised Evan Hunt didn't put you up in the corporate suite at the Omni."

Cassie attempted to breathe normally. *Now they were discussing Evan Hunt?* Jewel shrugged with ease and said, "Perhaps it's already occupied. And we're very happy with our rooms."

"How come you're not sitting at one of the Princess tables?" another gentleman asked, brow slightly knit.

"One of the what?" Cassie replied, trying very hard to keep her voice light as she swiped a cloth napkin across her lips.

"The Princess Cosmetics tables, of course," he replied, pointing toward the front of the room.

Cassie's head shot around to look, her gaze landing instantly on the smiling and still unbelievably handsome face of Evan Hunt himself.

Chapter Three

S HE SUCKED IN her breath involuntarily—
hyperventilation was near. She couldn't believe this.
He was here! Her heart fluttered and her stomach
churned as she studied him—a beautiful man amidst
other beautiful people.

He fit in this setting. And she didn't. It was that
simple. She fought the impulse to run, truly wishing she
could, but reacting that way would only make the
situation worse.

"Oh, I believe the seats were already taken," Jewel
coolly answered of the Princess tables. "And besides," she
winked with a secretive smile, "I think the company over
here is better."

To Cassie's unparalleled relief, Jewel's ploy worked.
The rich old people chuckled at her flattery and the
chitchat took a turn toward the stock market. Cassie
found herself admiring Jewel's smooth charm only
wished she could behave as confidently as her friend.
How would she ever stand a chance in the business world
when she got ruffled so easily? Still, thank God for

Jewel's quick wits.

The pop of a microphone quieted the gentle murmurs of conversation that blanketed the room and all eyes shifted toward the podium near Evan Hunt's table. Instead of watching the speaker, though, Cassie's gaze fell on Evan Hunt's handsome profile.

She listened to a blustery fellow thank everyone for showing their support for the homeless as she studied Evan Hunt's soft, dark hair and the strong cheekbones that defined his virile face. She heard the speaker thanking myriad people for coordinating the event as she wondered if it was possible that only hours ago she had peered into his eyes, breathed in his masculine scent, and actually touched his chest through the clothes he wore. It seemed like eons had elapsed since then, each passing second making her want him more even as their worlds seemed to grow farther and farther apart.

What was it about him? What drew her to him so strongly and made her react so dramatically? After all, there were other handsome men in the world. She passed by plenty of them every day on the busy Chicago streets.

But didn't every girl have some image in her mind— and heart—of her perfect man? Maybe running head on into someone who personified hers had just been too much to take. Or maybe it was because he was so unattainable—and she'd felt that. Painfully. Meeting her perfect man in a cotton candy pink uniform and old gym shoes, and then promptly showing him how inept she was at even the simplest of tasks, had felt like the ultimate humiliation.

There's so much more to me. And she wished that, somehow, she could have shown him. Even if it wouldn't have mattered at all in the big picture of life, she wished that, for just a moment, she could have made a good impression on him, could have earned a smile from him that hadn't resulted from pity.

The speaker concluded by officially opening the dance floor and instructing the D.J. to start the music. The lights fell low and a handful of eager people scurried to the rainbow-lighted floor as sounds of '70s disco filled the air. Cassie recognized the first old song as "Disco Inferno".

The older couples at Cassie's table took the opportunity to quickly excuse themselves, saying that they were calling it a night. Cassie stayed seated next to Jewel, barely able to mutter polite goodnights and nice-to-meet-yous, still completely stressed out that Evan Hunt was in the same room with her.

When the couples had departed, Cassie glared at Jewel. Stress had helped her make a decision. "I'm leaving," she said.

Jewel turned on her with wide eyes. "Leaving? Why on earth would you do that?"

"Are you serious?"

Jewel nodded, looking sincere.

So apparently Cassie would have to spell this out. "Okay, for one thing, you've made a verbal connection between us and Princess Cosmetics. A connection that, may I remind you, does not exist. If any of those people choose to say something to Evan Hunt before they leave, we're caught in a silly lie. Therefore, I think we should get out while we still can."

"Relax," Jewel said with her usual easy shrug. "They said they were going home. I'm sure they're all headed out the door and climbing into their Rolls Royces by now."

Cassie didn't feel even slightly reassured. And in fact, Jewel had been so calm and cool about Evan Hunt's presence here that it suddenly made Cassie wonder… "You knew about this, didn't you?"

Jewel's eyes pleaded innocence. "Knew about what?"

"That he would be here." Cassie's stomach fluttered again at the mere reminder that he was right across the room from her.

Then Jewel lowered her eyelids before peeking up cautiously. "Okay, I might have had an inkling. But you would have, too, if you'd bothered to read the entire article. It said he was quite a philanthropist and was expected to be in attendance here tonight."

Cassie shook her head in frustration at this whole turn of events. A few hours ago she'd been a simple waitress, content to go home and soak her feet in a tub of warm water. Okay, she hadn't really been *content*, but at least she'd been relaxed, which was pretty much the opposite of how she felt at the moment.

"Well, this whole thing is still ridiculous," she said. "And I'm going home." She stood and grabbed her purse before stalking from the table.

"Hold it," Jewel said, close on her heels.

Cassie whirled to face her red-dressed friend. "Why?"

And Jewel spoke in a knowing voice. "You're only leaving because you're afraid of him."

Cassie glanced down at herself, masquerading as something, someone, she was not. Someone she could probably never be. Why bother denying the truth in Jewel's words? "Fine," she said. "I'm afraid of him. So what?"

"Are you crazy, Cass? This is your big chance with him! It's like fate or something. How can you pass that up?"

"I think *you're* the crazy one," Cassie replied. She glanced again at Evan Hunt, who stood nearby—*too* nearby for comfort—conversing with several elegant-looking people. Then she shifted her gaze back to Jewel and lowered her voice. "This whole set-up of yours is completely absurd. And this is *not* my big chance with him or anybody else. I mean, what would a guy like *that* want with *me*?"

She watched a small, devilish smile slowly grow on her friend's face. "I don't know," Jewel said, "but I think you're about to find out."

"What?"

"Don't look now, but he's coming this way."

Cassie's stomach went hollow and her knees grew weak. Surely he wasn't *really* coming this way, not toward *her*. He would walk right past and go speak to someone else. But if he *was* coming this way, *why*? To say, *Hey, I heard you were masquerading as someone connected with Princess Cosmetics?* Or, *Aren't you the waitress that ruined my clothes today?*

But before she could form another thought, he was standing beside her, looking handsome and sincere and perfect, and instead of saying either of the things she had imagined, he simply said, "Excuse me. May I have this dance?"

She pulled in her breath and realized she'd lost the ability to speak. This couldn't be happening. Because it simply didn't make sense.

She gazed up into what were still the greenest eyes she'd ever seen. They sparkled beneath the room's dimmed lighting in a way that made her dizzy. *But this is happening. To me. Cassie Turner, poverty-stricken waitress. Evan Hunt has just asked me to dance.*

Only then did she realize that the tempo of the music had slowed and that the first strains of Roberta Flack's "The First Time Ever I Saw Your Face"—possibly one of the most romantic songs of all time in her opinion—wafted through the air around them. Her entire body began to tingle.

Jewel nudged her ankle as she continued staring up into Evan Hunt's piercing emerald eyes. But she still had no luck finding any words. So she simply held up her hand, offering it to him, and he smiled at her silent acceptance. He led her to the dance floor as she cast a helpless look over her shoulder at Jewel, who grinned at her like a Cheshire Cat.

She still didn't think this could be real. But if it was a dream, it was a wonderful one. And for the first time since it had started, she didn't want to run away anymore. Evan Hunt was sliding his arms gently around her waist and she was lifting her hands tentatively to his strong shoulders, becoming lost in his gentle embrace.

She bit her lip nervously before summoning the courage to peek up at him again. And when she lifted her gaze to his, she experienced a flashback to earlier that day when she'd touched his tie. She wondered futilely if he was remembering it, too.

Yet the smile he bestowed on her then was clearly not the sympathetic gesture cast toward a bumbling waitress. "Thank you for dancing with me," he said gallantly.

She only nodded, her heart in her throat.

He peered down at her, his expression turning endearingly sheepish as the romantic music surrounded them. "I hope I didn't seem too forward."

"No," she blurted, finally locating her voice. "I mean, not at all."

"I just saw you standing there, looking like a vision in that dress, and I guess impulse grabbed me. I had a lousy day at the office and suppose I just wanted to dance with a beautiful woman."

Cassie inhaled deeply, trying to calm the frantic beating of her heart. Vision? Beautiful woman? Maybe this really *was* a dream. Did flesh and blood men actually say things like that? She didn't know how to react, yet luckily she didn't have to before he continued.

"But I don't want to bore you with my problems. Instead, maybe I should introduce myself. I'm Evan Hunt." He smiled. "And you are?"

Dumbstruck with lust.

She gazed up at him helplessly, repeating the same words over and over in her mind. *Thank you, God. Thank you, God.* He didn't recognize her.

Now she would only have to make sure she kept it that way. After all, if he didn't realize it himself, she certainly couldn't let him find out she was the clumsy waitress who had spilled tea all over him. His eyes had been gorgeous and full of understanding in the diner when she'd been ruining his lunch, but they were so much deeper, warmer, *now,* as they gazed at the *new* her. The her who had become a *vision,* a *beautiful woman.* Just for this night, she decided, she would be someone else. She would be… "Cassandra," she finally replied. "Cassandra Turner."

He smiled. "Pretty name, Cassandra."

She blushed, wondering how surprised he'd be to know she'd just made it up. The name on her birth certificate was actually Catherine, but that just didn't sound sophisticated enough for the moment.

"Great song," he said then, and she felt an instant kinship with him.

"Yes," she replied, smiling up into his eyes. "It is. A favorite of my mother's."

A spine-tingling moment of slightly awkward silence

filled the air until Evan Hunt grinned down at her. "I guess this is where we make small talk, Cassandra. So, tell me, what do you do?"

Wait on tables, socialize with the homeless, attack businessmen with glasses of iced tea. "Well," she began, swallowing heavily and getting her game face fully on, "I'm between positions right now. But I'm interested in business administration."

He nodded and Cassie wondered if her answer was okay.

"Where did you go to school?" he asked.

She began to answer Hargrove High, when suddenly it didn't sound right. "Har...vard," she said instead, mentally kicking herself as the disjointed word left her mouth.

Evan Hunt raised his eyebrows. "Harvard Business School, huh? Impressive."

Cassie nodded and glanced down at his collar, unable to look him in the eye. Impressive, indeed.

"So, where are you from, Cassandra Turner?"

The backwoods of Kentucky? No, despite the certain charms of her hometown, it just didn't have the right ambiance for the moment. She thought quickly, remembering she still carried a hint of a southern accent. "Atlanta," she confidently replied. She'd heard good things about Atlanta. And most people this far north wouldn't know the difference between an Atlanta accent and a Kentucky one.

Evan tilted his head slightly. "You're one of the

Turners of Atlanta?"

"Sure," she said. Then realized he must be referring to some rich vein of people who happened to bear her last name, and good Lord, what if he knew them personally? "I mean no," she corrected. "Which is to say...we're not that closely related."

He grinned. "So I'm not dancing Ted Turner's granddaughter around the floor then?"

Oh, *those* Turners. The CNN/TBS/Atlanta Braves Turners. She swallowed. "Afraid not. We're...uh...second cousins."

Geez, where was she getting this stuff? Her heart beat a mile a minute—though not only from passion now, but also from the tension of telling lies. And not just telling them—it felt more like she was *spewing* them. She'd never had the need to tell many lies before, and she'd probably told more of them to Evan Hunt in the last three minutes than she'd told to anyone in her entire life. Time to change the subject to something she could discuss without fear.

"Are you a large supporter of the homeless?" she asked.

Evan's eyes turned sympathetic. "Yes, my company makes regular donations to some of the shelters in the city."

She nodded. "That's wonderful."

"You?" he asked.

"Yes," she replied as they continued swaying to the music. "Although my contributions are a little smaller."

"Oh?"

"Well, I help out at the Sunshine House every weekend."

Evan Hunt's eyes grew wide with admiration. "That's not a small thing at all, Cassandra."

"I don't do much," she insisted, giving a slight shake of her head. "Serve meals and help clean up a little. I wish I had the resources to donate money, but…" She stopped, suddenly remembering that she was Cassandra from Atlanta. "But being between positions, I've had to put myself on a budget."

He smiled and pulled back just enough to give her an appreciative once-over. "I'm glad you budgeted enough for this dress," he said. "It's gorgeous on you."

Warmth flooded her cheeks, her body tingling in all the right places beneath his gaze. Oh my, but he knew how to make her feel good. "Thank you," she whispered.

As the last notes of the love song faded into silence, Evan Hunt's strong arms started to loosen around her. Oh God, it was over already? The song, the moment, his embrace, had all ended—that fast. She gazed up at him, wondering if he could see the simple longing in her eyes, wondering if he could see the simple country girl hiding behind the expensive clothes and elegant hairstyle.

"Thank you for the dance, Cassandra," he said. The deep timbre of his voice curled her toes and assured her that her secret was safe.

"It was my pleasure," she said, her voice coming out breathier than intended.

He gave his head a slight tilt, his eyes shining with—if she wasn't mistaken—flirtation. "Maybe we could…get together later. For another dance."

She instantly began nodding, hoping she didn't appear too eager. Then she watched him back away from her through the crowd, murmuring to himself, "Maybe this day wasn't so rotten after all."

When he finally disappeared in the sea of people that spilled onto the dance floor with the return of the disco beat, Cassie was both disappointed to be alone and grateful for a chance to catch her breath.

What an incredibly hot man. How kind. How utterly charming.

And how she had *lied* to him! Over and over again! Okay, maybe it had only been two or three times, but it had felt like more.

And they'd been such *stupid* lies. And such *big* lies.

Still, she'd had to do something to try to fit into his world. She couldn't exactly have explained that the dress was borrowed and that her hair was usually much flatter and that she was employed at Fast Eddie's Diner on Randolph under the "L".

"I saw you dancing with Evan Hunt."

Cassie spun to see a young woman moving to the beat of "Y.M.C.A." She wore a black lace dress, and the diamonds around her slim neck glistened as she danced. Her dark hair hung in dramatic waves and dipped over one eye. These were the people of Evan Hunt's world.

"Yes," Cassie replied as she joined in the dancing.

"You're lucky," the girl said. "He's a dream."

Cassie nodded. That, he was.

Then the girl glanced toward the D.J. "This retro music is wild."

Cassie nodded again, then gathered the courage to attempt further conversation. She decided to stick to something simple. "Yeah—the Village People are always still fun, right?"

The girl in the black lace hesitated. "Hmm…" After thinking about it for what Cassie deemed a ridiculously long time, the girl finally replied. "I never really thought of them as fun, but I can appreciate both Kerouac and Ginsberg."

"Ginsberg, huh?" Cassie said. She'd never known any of their real names. "I liked the construction worker myself. It's that illusion of sweat, you know what I mean? Sexy. But you know what I never got? The Indian. The rest are professions, but where does the Indian fit in? I've never known anyone to be a professional Indian."

The elegant girl tilted her head, her hair falling even farther over her eye, and the one eye Cassie could see looked a little perplexed. She began to get the impression that somehow they weren't quite on the same page and that maybe she should shut up. In fact, she should probably *leave*. She didn't belong here, after all. And a romantic dance with a gorgeous man didn't change that.

Where's Jewel? She panned the room as she danced, deciding she was definitely going to let her friend have it for not letting her leave when she'd wanted to. Now she'd danced with this man, she'd lied to this man, and she'd fallen in...

She gasped. Had she? Fallen in love? Could it happen that quickly?

Certainly not.

And still she had the nagging feeling that it might be true.

She'd heard of love at first sight, after all. And she'd been waiting twenty-five years for love of *any* kind to hit her. She was certainly no expert on the subject, but...

That was when the warmth of a body moved in close behind her, along with strong hands that slid delicately around her slender waist. And normally, an unexpected embrace would have made her leap out of her skin, but somehow she recognized his touch. She glanced over her shoulder and nearly shuddered at the beautiful nearness of his face. "Hi," he said, his voice low and sexy.

"Hi," she whispered.

"I hope you don't mind my coming back so soon, but I couldn't stay away."

She pulled in her breath. "You couldn't?"

He shook his head, moving in rhythm with her to the music. "I've had a couple of glasses of wine and so I'll just be honest," he said. "I watched you dancing from across the room and couldn't take my eyes off you. I wanted to be close to you again."

Oh. My. Yes, this was a *very* good dream.

And somehow then, her body took over and she felt herself involuntarily begin to lean back against him, melt into him, begin to become a part of his sweet warmth…just before he pulled unexpectedly away.

She whirled to face him, again disappointed by the loss of his touch—only to find him grinning at her as he used his arms to spell out the letters Y-M-C-A along with the rest of the crowd. She joined in, laughing as they danced.

Maybe it wasn't so hard to be part of his world at all—especially if he was easy-going and fun like this.

And so the dancing continued to the parade of '70s hits. She couldn't believe how much fun she had as one song faded into another and then into another. Not only was Evan Hunt handsome and sexy, and sweet and kind, but he was also one heck of a good time. She almost forgot that only moments ago one confusing conversation with one sophisticated society girl had nearly sent her running away. It seemed that every time Evan came near her, it helped push her doubts aside.

Because I'm Cassandra. And Cassandra didn't have to be afraid. Because Cassandra was part of his world. Cassandra was everything he wanted.

So she tried to forget who she *really* was as she danced with him. And each time a negative thought found its way into her mind, she swiftly shoved it away with one glance into those gorgeous green eyes.

It was only a shame that the dress and the shoes had to go back to the store, that she would awaken with flat hair, and that essentially all this would end at midnight when the dance was over. *But that's tomorrow—you can at least keep having fun tonight.* The thought—one she knew would make Jewel proud—inspired her to shove those others aside and get back to the business of dancing with Evan.

Occasionally they left the dance floor for drinks and, once, a bathroom break, but otherwise it was non-stop dancing and togetherness. And of course her favorite dances were the occasional slow ones that allowed her to be closer to him again.

A few minutes before twelve, Evan excused himself for a moment, leaving her on the dance floor alone. Suddenly without him there, she felt strangely adrift in the sea of people that surrounded her. Tonight she had been one of them, but without Evan at her side, she immediately felt foreign in their midst.

And she wondered again where Jewel was—she hadn't seen her in hours. She was anxious to tell her friend everything that had happened—and yet she dreaded the train ride home, knowing that the fantasy would be over and she'd be heading back to the big, empty warehouse apartment alone.

"There you are." Evan's warm grasp closed on her arm and she turned to face him. His face had grown slightly damp with sweat from dancing, and the hair that hung haphazardly over his forehead was wet with perspiration, as well. Cassie recalled her conversation with the society girl earlier—how she'd explained about the illusion of sweat turning her on—and looking at Evan now proved that it was true. And he was no illusion. She wanted him madly. Whether she fit into his world or not.

"Where'd you go?" she asked, smiling shyly. "I thought I'd been abandoned."

"Never."

Then she heard the first strains of a familiar tune, one she'd already heard earlier tonight. "I had to go request a song," he rasped, leaning near her ear. He planted a soft kiss high on her cheek before pulling back to look at her. "The First Time Ever I Saw Your Face" filled the air once more and Cassie's heart shuddered.

All thought fled as her body melted into his, liquefying in his grasp, and as her lips involuntarily lifted, reaching, until they found his warm mouth.

His kiss, which started light and gentle, soon became warmer and deeper as his tongue pushed its way between her lips. Rainbow lights swirled around them and she had the sensation of floating on air.

Dizziness gripped her as the kiss finally ended.

She slowly opened her eyes to discover that the world hadn't changed much in the last few moments—music still played, couples still danced around them, and time hadn't stopped. But *she* had changed. She'd never been kissed like that before. She'd never felt so completely saturated and engulfed by a man. And she knew she would never be the same.

"When can I see you again?" he asked, his voice low and tinged with passion.

"Um, um…" Somehow, even still, she hadn't seen

that coming, hadn't thought that far ahead.

He laughed softly. "I hope that means soon."

She smiled and nodded, then let Evan pull her back into his arms as the romantic song played on. Being pressed against him—her arms locked around his neck, his clasped at her waist—made her feel safe, and complete. And in love.

Even as absolutely crazy as that sounded, even to her.

How did this happen? How did this absolutely amazing night, with this amazing man, ending with this amazing kiss, really happen? To me.

She could only chalk it up to one thing—fate. She'd heard the word more than once today. From Mac. From Jewel. And she'd thought it was ridiculous. But now it was the only explanation that made any sense.

When the romantic song ended and the clock on the wall read midnight, the D.J. brought the party to a close, reminding everyone to drive safely. But Evan didn't let go of her. Even when the lights came up and people began to disperse, he still held her tight.

Only when she was beginning to believe he might hold onto her forever did he finally release his grip, and she again experienced the painful separation of their bodies. Knowing that the night had come to an end made it extra hard for her to let go.

"Guess this is it," he said somberly, gazing down at her.

"Guess so," she replied.

He reached into his jacket to pull out a pen, then

grabbed a tiny square napkin from a now-vacant table nearby. "Will you give me your number?"

Nervously, Cassie relayed her phone number, noting his thick scrawl of the name *Cassandra* on the paper.

"Is it okay to call any time?" he asked.

It was a trickier question than he could have guessed. "My daytime schedule is kind of hectic," she replied, wincing at having to tell yet another fib to this wonderful man. Still, she couldn't exactly take phone calls at Fast Eddie's.

"Even while you're between jobs?"

"I'm...uh...interviewing," she claimed. "A lot."

He nodded knowingly. "I forgot I was dealing with an ambitious woman. So there's no way to reach you during the day?"

"How about it I call *you*?" she suggested, the words spilling from her lips out of desperation.

Evan reached again into his jacket and this time pulled out a business card that bore the Princess logo, along with his name, company address, and phone number. "Don't be shy about using this," he told her, placing it in her hand.

She smiled up at him as the lights lifted. "It's been a wonderful night," she whispered.

He leaned in to kiss her forehead, smiled his agreement, then turned to go.

Cassie couldn't believe it. It was too good to be true. The night was ending, but the fantasy wasn't.

Chapter Four

EARLY THE NEXT morning Cassie bumped into Jewel in the back room at Eddie's as their shift was about to begin. It was sobering to see her friend back in her pink uniform, no longer decked out in red sequins, and even more sobering to glance in the mirror and see her own pink dress and flat hair pulled unceremoniously back into its usual ponytail.

"You all right?" Jewel asked. "You look a little sick."

Cassie sighed, plopping down in one of the plastic chairs behind the break table. "Just depressed, I guess. Or feeling guilty. Or scared to death."

Jewel blinked. "What did I miss?" Cassie hadn't seen her after leaving Evan last night. She'd found a note at their table indicating that Jewel had found a CEO of her own and they were going back to his place.

"I wish you wouldn't have run out on me. I could have used your help," Cassie explained.

Jewel replied with a lascivious grin. "Seems I was in high demand last night."

But Cassie could only sigh. "Jewel, I've got big problems."

"Spill," Jewel encouraged her, pulling out a chair beside her.

So Cassie then proceeded to pour out the evening's events, one by one, each lie she'd told stacked upon the next like a delicate tower of cards.

When she finished, Jewel mulled it all over for a moment, assessing the situation, until she announced, "You know, the lying isn't the most urgent problem here."

Cassie blinked her surprise. "No?"

"No," Jewel said. "It's the calling."

"What do you mean?"

"You've taken a guy responsibility and thrown it on yourself," Jewel explained. "You can't call too soon or you'll look too needy, too anxious. On the other hand, you can't wait too long. You've got to think like a guy. You've got to play it cool."

Cassie sighed. She hadn't thought of that. She hadn't been thinking clearly about *any* of this. "What if he asks me to go to some fancy event?" she asked desperately, thinking ahead.

"Well, depending upon where you're going, maybe I can get Irma to lend you another dress."

"This is going to be constant scheming," Cassie concluded glumly, shaking her head. "What have I done?"

"I don't know why you didn't just tell him who you were in the first place," Jewel offered.

And Cassie admitted, "I don't really know either. But

I guess it's the same reason we fibbed to the people at our table last night. I just wanted to feel good enough, worthy. I just want to fit in with his life."

And in retrospect, the truth would have been relatively easy. Probably easier than lying had been. But the truth wasn't so easy now.

So she'd just have to tough this out and hope that maybe he'd lose interest in her quickly.

Of course, she'd die then.

But at least her lie would be safe.

She sighed yet again, realizing that she probably just wasn't meant to be with such a classy guy.

Jewel cast her a sympathetic smile. "You'll be okay, Cass. This will work itself out. You've got to have faith."

Sheesh, they were back to that again? "Faith in what?"

Jewel tilted her head, smile still in place. "Fate, of course. It wouldn't have brought Prince Charming into your path if something good wasn't supposed to happen."

Cassie weighed the thought. "Well, if something good was supposed to happen, I've probably screwed it up with all my lying." And now she wanted to change the subject, tired of dwelling on her guilt. "So who were you with last night?"

"Oh, Malcolm? He's the CEO of Warwick Foods. You know, they make all those fancy gift packs with cheeses and caviar and things."

"Wow," Cassie said, letting her eyes widen appreciatively.

"What are you *wow*ing? You've got your own CEO," Jewel pointed out.

Cassie gave her friend a matter-of-fact look. "But I'm guessing you didn't string yours a line of lies that could stretch from here to Kentucky."

"True," Jewel said. "Malcolm knows the truth about me, that I'm just a poor waitress hoping to make it big in the hair industry someday. But there's a big difference between my CEO and yours."

"What's that?"

"Mine is just a fling," Jewel said. "A passing tryst. Nothing serious."

Something in the very idea disappointed Cassie a little. "You're not planning on seeing him again?"

"Well, I am. But just for fun." Jewel grinned. "I'd never have guessed it, but Malcolm's got a Harley. And he can't wait to see me in leather." Yet then she let out a wistful sigh, growing serious again. "Still, it's nothing like what you've got going on in your heart for Evan Hunt."

Cassie cast her friend a critical glance. "How do you know what I've got going on in my heart?"

A glint of wisdom shone in Jewel's eyes as she said, "You can lie with your mouth, Cassie, but not with your eyes."

EVAN HUNT PICKED up coffee and donuts at the bakery

near his building before walking to work. He usually didn't eat breakfast, and he usually didn't walk to work, but the weather was beautiful this morning.

He strolled through the pink marble lobby, barely feeling the floor beneath his feet. "Morning, Carl," he said to the security guard. Carl hesitated, then offered a friendly smile and tipped his hat. Only then did Evan realize that he didn't usually say hello to Carl and probably hadn't in years.

He stepped onto the elevator, offering greetings to the young woman who had held the door when she'd seen his approach. But as the elevator rose, it was a different woman who invaded his mind. Cassandra Turner. He couldn't conceal his smile.

She was so shy, and so sweet. A certain innocence colored her demeanor, but underneath he'd sensed a quiet confidence that appealed. Something about her seemed familiar, but he couldn't say from where. Probably just his imagination.

Or maybe…this was what it was like to fall in love. Maybe when you found the right person, they had that quality of familiarity, that quality of being someone that you've been looking for all along.

Love, though? Damn—was he really thinking about *love*? Seemed highly impractical for a man in his position.

A thousand aspects of a failing company weighed on his mind—how on earth had the concept of love started creeping in? Only yesterday, after all, women— romance—had been the last thing on his agenda. Now, suddenly, they were the first. But not women in general. Only one pervaded his thoughts.

The ding of the elevator delivered him to his penthouse office. He stepped briskly off the elevator to find Miriam sitting behind her desk looking distressed.

"Why the frown, Miriam?"

"I was starting to get worried," she said. "You're never this late. It's almost 8:30."

He smiled. "I slept in an extra half hour. And I picked up some breakfast." With that he lowered a white wax bag onto her desk. "Hope you like glazed."

"Why, Evan Hunt," she said, her eyes beginning to twinkle, "what on earth has gotten into you? I haven't seen you in this good of a mood in ages." Then she tilted her head. "Maybe not ever."

Evan hesitated, then chose not to answer, heading for his office.

"You met a girl, didn't you?" Miriam asked slyly behind him.

Wow. He stopped, looked back at her. How did she know? Was he really that transparent? Or did she just truly know him that well?

The older woman's giggle sounded almost girlish—before her smile turned as sly as a TV detective's. "Evan Hunt, I've known you since you were a little boy and I've never seen you with this look."

"What look is that, Mir?"

And her eyes fairly danced with light as she said, "The look of love."

THE MORNING DRAGGED by for Cassie. But at least she didn't spill anything on anybody. Her mind was elsewhere. And not in a good place. All she could think of was guilt. And worry.

When her lunch break finally arrived, she couldn't eat. "I'll nibble on something when I get back," she told Jewel. "I've got an important errand to run."

Then she walked to the post office, Evan Hunt's new tie tucked beneath her arm. Late last night she'd cut up a generic shopping bag and wrapped the tie box in the brown paper, sealing it with packing tape. Then she'd referred to the pink business card Evan had given her, printing his address on the outside.

She'd hoped she would feel better returning from the post office, that perhaps shipping the tie off would somehow ease her mind and put at least the circumstances of their meeting to rest. But, to her dismay, she didn't feel better at all. And she trudged all the way back to Fast Eddie's knowing there was only one thing to do.

"Don't try to talk me out of it, Jewel," she said, stomping into the back room.

Jewel looked up from the greasy hamburger she ate. "Talk you out of what?"

"I'm calling him."

"You can't!" Jewel protested, heavily outlined eyes widening. "It's way too soon!"

"That doesn't matter," Cassie explained. "I'm calling

him to tell him the truth. I can't go on like this, being dishonest. It's eating me alive."

Jewel lowered her chin, then attempted reason. "Cassie, think this through."

"I have, and it's the only solution." She nodded succinctly. "And I knew you would try to talk me out of it, which is why I just told you not to. So I don't want to hear another word about it, okay? All I want is your silent moral support. From the other room," she added.

Jewel paused, as if deciding whether or not to keep arguing. And she wisely chose not to, but her eyes warned of impending disaster as she quietly rose from the table and vacated the break room.

"Thank you," Cassie said behind her. Then she boldly picked up the phone and dialed the number on the business card.

"Princess Cosmetics. Evan Hunt's office."

"Could I speak to Mr. Hunt, please?"

"Who's calling please?"

Cassie swallowed. "Cassandra Turner."

"CASSANDRA TURNER ON line one for you, Evan," Miriam's voice sang knowingly over the intercom.

And to his utter astonishment, Evan's heart began to pound. He hadn't dreamed she would call him this soon. He'd planned to call her himself tonight from home, but he was thrilled that she'd beat him to it.

He picked up the receiver. "Cassandra?"

No answer. He could only hear the sounds of dishes clattering and jumbled conversations somewhere in the distance. And then he thought he heard her breathing. It sounded labored. "Cassandra, are you there?"

"Um...yes," she said. "Sorry. I'm here."

His heart flooded at the sound of her voice. "I'm glad you called," he told her.

"You are?"

She still sounded so sweet and timid and nervous, and he wanted to put her at ease. "Of course I am. I'd planned to call you myself later."

"Oh." It came out on a soft, quiet breath and the fluttery quality in her voice made him want her wildly. "Evan," she said, "I called because I wanted to tell you..."

"What?" he asked when her voice trailed off.

"Well, that I..."

"Yes?" Her hesitation was killing him.

"That I...had a lovely time last night."

He smiled with relief. There for a second it had sounded as if something bad was coming. "I had a lovely evening, too, Cassandra."

Her breath started fluttering again, and even as adorable a trait as he found it, he decided to change the subject, still hoping to help her relax and feel comfortable talking to him. "Where are you?" he asked. "What's all that noise I hear?"

"Um, I'm in a restaurant."

"Maybe I can meet you there for a late lunch," he

suggested.

"No," she said quickly. "I mean, I already ate, and I'm…in a hurry. Late for an interview."

"I should have figured," he said, grinning to himself. "Can we get together later, then?"

She hesitated. "Um…okay."

"Do you run?"

"Do I run?"

"Yeah," he said. "I run most nights along the lakefront. I was just thinking that if you happened to be a runner, too, maybe we could go running together. But if you don't run, no problem. We can go for a walk. Or out to dinner. Or anything you want."

"Running's fine," she said. "I love to run."

"Really? Great! Can I pick you up?"

"Um, no," she said. "I'm going to be busy for the rest of the day, so I'll meet you."

"All right. Say, seven o'clock? In Grant Park at the corner of Jackson and Lakeshore?"

"Sounds good," she said. "See you then."

RUNNING'S FINE? I love to run?

Cassie stood in the break room after hanging up the phone, wanting to kick herself.

She had never gone running before in her life, but from all she'd heard about it, it was strenuous. It called for being in shape. It demanded stamina. It required cute exercise clothes. Unfortunately, she possessed none of these things.

She had no idea why she'd agreed to go running when she could have opted for a nice leisurely walk or, better yet, a good restaurant and maybe a movie. The words had just popped out of her before she could think clearly. Running sounded like such a hip thing to do. She'd seen lots of people jogging along the path by Lakeshore Drive and they exuded a certain image—confidence and physical fitness combined with a certain understated upwardly-mobile-urban thing: successful people who were not afraid to sweat in front of each other. She didn't know if anyone else viewed these city runners in the same light as she did, but nonetheless, these people had something she wanted, presented an image she found appealing, and if Evan was a part of it, then apparently she wanted to be a part of it, too. No matter how silly or improbable it seemed.

But now you have to start thinking rationally.

Well, a little bit anyway.

Honesty—*that* had been a rational plan. But somehow it had fallen by the wayside. *You really need to get control of your mouth when communicating with this man. As in stop saying the exact opposite of what you* should *be saying every time you talk to him.*

But for now she had to think smartly and rationally—within the context of running.

It would be impossible to acquire physical stamina in the next few hours, but perhaps *not* so impossible to at least get some attractive sportswear. And maybe if she looked cute enough, Evan wouldn't even notice her inept running capabilities. After all, he'd sounded thrilled to hear from her. And despite everything, her heart grew lighter at the thought—it had grown lighter just hearing his deep, sexy voice. Maybe somehow, in the end, none of this terrible deception would matter.

Jewel stuck her head in the room. "Is the coast clear? Did you call him?"

Cassie nodded.

"And?"

"And we're going running tonight at seven."

Jewel's eyes lit up in surprise. "Great! Do you want to borrow some of my sexy gym clothes?"

"I tried to tell him the truth, Jewel—really," Cassie explained.

"Do you want something that conceals or something that flatters?"

"But I just couldn't do it," she went on. "Not when he sounded so happy to hear from me.

"You're so tiny and slim," Jewel said, "I'd suggest going the flattering route."

"So now I've just buried myself deeper, too deep to possibly dig my way out." Cassie slumped in the chair where she sat and slowly lifted her eyes to her friend. "Do you think I'm awful?"

"No. I just think we need to talk about your hair."

"I mean, every now and then," Cassie said, "doesn't someone need to do something impulsive? Something a little risky, a little reckless?"

"Yes, but neglecting your hair would be a serious mistake at this juncture in the relationship."

"Jewel, I've always worked hard to be a good person. And look at me now. This is the worst thing I've ever done."

Jewel sat down. "*This* is the worst thing you've ever done, Cass?"

She nodded.

"No offense, kid, but in the sin department, this is nothing. If this is the worst thing you've ever done, then give yourself a break and milk it for all it's worth."

Cassie couldn't help feeling completely disheartened by Jewel's words. She wished Jewel would scold her, tell her it was wrong, encourage her to fix it before it got any further out of hand.

"Well, it may not sound like a big deal to you, but it is to me. And Jewel, it's just that…he's so wonderful. And I would never want to hurt him."

"Listen—it's way too soon to worry about hurting the guy. Or to assume he's wonderful just because he seems that way so far. It's early days here yet, so just trust me. If the time comes to tell him, you'll tell him."

Cassie widened her gaze on her friend. "But *how* will I tell him? How will I tell him without looking like a completely fake, dishonest, manipulative loser?" Guilt continued to pummel her, so matter *what* Jewel said.

"You'll find a way. And he'll understand." Jewel sounded so sure.

But Cassie rolled her eyes. "Easy for you to say."

TONI BLAKE

"Life generally has a way of working things out for the best, Cassie," her friend insisted, doing the wise woman thing again.

And Cassie countered, "Tell that to Mac."

Jewel simply let out a *harrumph*, then gave her a threatening look, hands on hips. "If you don't quit being so negative, I'll make you run in something ugly."

Cassie's eyes widened at the horror of it. "You wouldn't?"

"No, of course I wouldn't," Jewel confessed, going softer again. "Now, with your coloring, I'm thinking of something with a splash of pink accented with an appropriately colored pony-tail holder. And I'll floof up your bangs before you leave."

Chapter Five

C ASSIE STOOD AT the corner of Jackson and Lakeshore, waiting. She felt ridiculous in Jewel's low-cut sports bra and a pair of hot pink leggings. She'd seen other girls wear that sort of thing, but it just wasn't her style. She'd never dreamed she'd don such apparel herself, let alone do it in public. "Won't people stare at me?" she'd asked Jewel, turning to study her rear end in the mirror at home.

"That's the idea," Jewel had told her.

And people *were* staring at her. Only she wasn't sure if the gazes were admiring or critical, and she wasn't at all sure she'd made a good choice for her date with Evan. But it was too late to do anything about it now.

Her heart pumped with the anticipation of seeing him again. He'd held her in his arms only the previous night, but it seemed eons ago. It was one thing to dance all night beneath swirling lights where the din of loud music made it difficult to talk, but would the mood be as wonderful and easy between them now, without music or dance to spur conversation?

She thought again of her many lies. Would she have to tell still more of them tonight? She wished she could simply find the strength to tell him the truth, but as she'd told Mac earlier, she couldn't imagine what Evan would think of her when he found out she'd been dishonest. He'd probably decide she was some gold-digging bimbo who'd seen his picture in the paper and moved in for the kill. He'd have no idea that it all came back to those beautiful green eyes of his, they way they pierced her, held her in place, made her heart beat in a whole new way. He'd have no idea that her lies had sprung simply from how much she wanted to be a part of his life.

She barely recognized the man jogging toward her in the crosswalk. He wore loose running shorts and a gray T-shirt that gave Cassie her first glimpse of the body beneath the business suit. The sight of his sinewy arms, glistening with sweat, nearly took her breath away. And tonight he had a sexy five o'clock shadow that made him appear rugged and aloof. She wouldn't have believed it was Evan Hunt if she hadn't seen that wayward lock of hair dipping over those captivating eyes.

"Hello there," he said, pushing the lock of hair back over his head and offering a smile that melted her.

"Hi." It came out sounding like a whisper. "I mean, *hi*," she said again, louder, trying to sound confident and more direct and like she didn't feel ridiculous in her outfit.

"Been waiting long?" he asked. He spoke with labored breath—he'd obviously already been running awhile.

"No," she replied. "Just got here."

"You look great," he said appreciatively.

Oh, sweet relief! Heat climbed her cheeks as she realized she shouldn't have worried so much, and she uttered the first words that came to mind. "So do you."

Oh no. Had she actually just said that? Oh God.

But Evan just gave an easy laugh that put her quickly at ease.

And when the light changed and the *Walk* signal lit up, he took her hand and led her back across the street toward the running path that bordered Lake Michigan. Along the way, they began to chat more at random. About what the beautiful day had been and what a warm, mild night it seemed to be turning into. About the kites people flew in the distance. About a passing a sailboat on Lake Michigan in the distance.

And out of the blue, something suddenly turned magical for her. Maybe it was just in her imagination—she'd heard love could do crazy things to a person. Or perhaps the aura of the night simply took over, filling her with the perfection she thought she might experience if she were really the person she pretended to be.

But suddenly—at least in those moments—she began to feel more at ease with him, to realize they were looking at the world through the same eyes and saw the same things, felt the same night air. She began to realize...this *was* real. And just walking hand in hand with him on a typical summer night felt way more than typical, and far closer to amazing.

Couples, both young and old, strolled past her and Evan, arm in arm. Other people walked dogs or sat nearby reading books or merely taking in the view. Classical music from a summer concert in the Pertrillo Bandshell wafted through the air, and the first hints of nightfall glistened on the water as the daylight began to dim. Cassie looked up into Evan's eyes, and then she remembered…

She had to run now. Uh-oh.

The magic faded a little with the sobering realization that the person she was pretending to be liked to exercise.

But you can do this.

"You set the pace," Evan told her as he broke into a gentle jog. She took a deep breath and fell in beside him, wondering for the first time in her life if she ran like a girl.

Slow and easy, she presumed, was the way to go here. *Preserve stamina. Save energy.* So she lifted her feet from the ground one after the other, falling into a slow, methodical groove as Evan ran alongside.

"So, lots of interviews for the aspiring young businesswoman today?"

She'd thought she'd been doing well, but when she opened her mouth to speak, her voice left her in mere gasps. "Yes," she breathed at him. "Lots."

"Anything interesting?"

She tried valiantly to summon the air from her lungs

to form more words. "Well...I...um..." But that was all
that came out, and maybe it was just as well since she
didn't exactly have any good answers anyway.

Though she sensed Evan still, understandably, waiting for an answer, and with her chest aching now as they
ran, she finally gave up and simply shook her head. She
heard her own breath, heavy now in the night air. Her
chest suddenly hurt a lot worse and she hoped it
wouldn't cave in. She wondered if she could be one of
those people who had a heart attack at a freakishly young
age.

"Are you okay?" Evan asked her, still jogging. For a
guy who'd been running awhile even before they'd met
up, he still looked devastatingly sexy and sounded
perfectly at ease when he spoke.

Just then, she stumbled over a small rise in the path
where they ran. "Ow!" she screeched as her body jolted
to a halt after the misstep, but she knew the clumsiness
was a godsend.

Evan stopped, too, placing a warm hand on her bare
shoulder. The touch tingled all through her like a
welcome little jolt of electricity. "Easy there. Are you all
right?"

"Just stubbed my toe," Cassie told him, finally catching her breath.

His smile held sympathy, much like the day before
when she'd spilled iced tea on him. But she also thought
she saw the hint of a question lurking there.

"To be completely honest with you," she added, "I

haven't run...in a while." *Like never.* But she left that last part out. Because lying had become her forte over the last two days. It was getting way too easy.

Easier than the truth apparently—because every time she attempted *that*, something else came out instead.

As Evan's smile widened, she wondered if the weakness that overtook her was from physical exertion or the wish to physically exert herself *with him*.

"That's okay," he told her. "Let's walk for a while."

What a relief. Walking she could handle.

"So tell me about these interviews you've been going on."

Of course, walking was more conducive to talking, and that could be a problem. "What would you like to know?"

He laughed. "I wasn't interrogating you. I was just curious where you're interviewing."

"Of course," she said, pretending to laugh along with him. Then she named a couple of well-known Chicago companies that she knew little about, but which sounded prestigious—all the while praying they weren't places Evan had any big connections he was offer to utilize on her behalf.

"What did you think of them?" he asked.

She bit her lip, concocting an answer. "Good benefits," she finally replied. "But not enough responsibility."

Evan laughed. "Want to take control, do you?"

But what she really wanted was simply to change the subject. "What about you?" she asked. "How was *your* day?"

Evan scowled at the question, but quickly adjusted his expression back to the pleasant one she'd quickly come to know. "Sorry," he said. "I don't want to take out my frustrations on you."

"I don't mind," she assured him. "But I'll admit, I'm a little surprised."

He raised his eyebrows, silently asking why.

She shrugged. "Guess I thought life was charmed at Princess Cosmetics."

Her companion hesitated only a second before shaking his head slightly. "Charmed would be...an exaggeration."

"Oh?" She tilted her head, sincerely curious. And truly a bit taken aback to find she was wrong.

"Well," he said then, clearly attempting to lighten his tone, "let's just say things could always be better." But a troubled look still lurked beneath his smile.

"Didn't I just read in the paper something about acquisitions?" she asked. "How could things get better than that?"

"Acquisitions are good, Cassandra," he replied, "but as I'm sure you know, it doesn't always mean business is booming."

"And it isn't?" She didn't mean to pry, but she found herself wanting to truly know this man, and given he was at the helm of the company, whatever was happening with it probably affected him deeply. She only hoped he didn't start talking about grosses and nets and profit margins and things she hadn't had a chance to learn about yet.

"Sales…could use a boost," he said simply.

And again, she couldn't help being surprised. "Really? I mean, you've got the biggest displays in the department stores. And Princess Cosmetics has been around all my life." She neglected to tell him that, due to their price tag, she'd never had the opportunity to own any of them. "So I always just assumed…"

Evan sighed. "It all goes back to my mother's death, almost ten years ago. She was the brains behind the business. Sure, Dad and his staff handled the financial stuff, but frankly, that's easy when the money is rolling in. Mom knew what women wanted—she seemed to have her finger on the pulse of women everywhere. She was really incredible." Evan's eyes lit up when he spoke of his mother in a way Cassie found endearing. "Anyway," he concluded, "it's…difficult to keep up the pace when the backbone of the company is gone."

Cassie sighed, thinking about the problem. Yes, it caught her off guard to hear that Princess Cosmetics weren't selling as well as they once had, and yet…now that she knew, it almost made sense to her.

"What?" Evan asked.

"What what?" she replied, lifting her eyes to his.

"You look like something's on your mind."

She shook her head half-heartedly.

"Really," he said, "tell me."

Cassie took a deep breath. She wanted to tread lightly, afraid to stick her opinion where it didn't belong—but he *was* insisting she answer. "Well, to be honest, Evan," she began, "I do find your products a little expensive. For the average woman, I mean. I know some women are willing to pay exorbitant amounts for makeup, but others aren't—or can't."

"What about you?" he asked.

"What *about* me?"

"What are you willing to pay for makeup? I hope that doesn't sound like a personal question, but I'm curious. You're obviously a woman with good taste and class. I'd like to know what you think."

Cassie considered the question. She couldn't tell him that she didn't like to pay over $6.98 for a tube of mascara, but she tried to look at it from Cassandra's viewpoint, mixing in a little of her own honesty.

"To tell you the the truth...I think many women may find Princess a little intimidating."

"What?" His jaw dropped, his shock written all over his face.

"Think about it," she said. "Cosmetics that have to be kept under glass? Cosmetics without price tags? We're not talking diamonds here—we're talking makeup. Personally, I like to be able to examine the merchandise a little. I like to flip over the bottle and read about the product. I like to hold different colors of foundation and blush and eye shadow in my hand, without a saleslady hovering over me. I like to be able to compare prices to see what I'm getting for my money."

Evan stayed quiet for a minute. "What you're saying makes sense," he told her. "But we have a certain image to uphold and we don't want our product line to be lumped in with the ones that hang on metal bars in drugstores."

Although that was exactly where Cassie bought all her makeup, she wasn't offended. She understood his point. Princess Cosmetics had represented glamour to her since she was a child. "I think there's a happy medium to be achieved," she simply replied.

"Hmm," he said, thinking. "I'd like to hear more about what you have in mind."

"Well, I don't have it in mind quite yet," she admitted. "I've never thought about this before right now. But I'll be happy to think about it some more if you'd like."

"I would," he said, nodding. "I'd like very much to hear whatever ideas you come up with."

"You'd be willing to take advice from a rookie?" she asked with playfully raised eyebrows.

And he smiled. "Not just any rookie. A Harvard Business School rookie."

Oh. God. She'd forgotten that part. In fact, over the past few minutes all her lies had faded to the back of her mind. Discussing her ideas with Evan had felt so very easy, genuine, real. Now the ugly truth had come back to slap her in the face.

"But enough talk about business," Evan said then.

And yeah, she had to agree that maybe another subject change was a good idea—for reasons Evan couldn't even begin to fathom. "What would you like to talk about?" she asked.

"Doesn't matter if we talk at all," he told her. "Just being with you is nice." Then he took her hand and led her along the lake's edge as the moon began to rise over the city, casting a pale path of light on the water's surface.

Cassie couldn't believe the electricity that traveled from Evan's hand up through her arm and out into her body. Of course, she'd felt it yesterday in the diner when she'd touched his chest through his clothing, and she'd felt it like crazy last night when they'd slow danced and he'd kissed her. But the sensation was somehow stronger now. Even though people moved up and down the walk on either side of them, Cassie felt as if they were alone, as if the moon shone on the water just for them. All thoughts of cosmetics and business and lies fell away from her. And the night regained some of the magic she'd felt earlier, before the running had started.

God, how she wanted this man. Body and soul. She still realized they'd just met, but she supposed that sometimes in life, you connected with someone quickly and emotions flowed in fast.

And walking in silence, neither of them feeling the need for conversation, gave her a chance to think, for the first time since all this had begun yesterday, about where it might lead. Into bed. And it gave her a chance to experience both the longing and the fear that such a possibility produced.

The longing, of course, was natural. But the fear—well, she could only blame that on her strict moral upbringing and the fact that no matter how hard she'd tried, she'd never managed to fall in love with Jimmy Hickson. If she'd ever fallen in love with her high school sweetheart, perhaps she would have slept with him, and perhaps the intimacy of sex wouldn't still be such a mystery. But as it was, Cassie had simply never found anyone who seemed important enough to have sex with.

She'd dated a few other guys after Jimmy, but she hadn't felt seriously about any of them, and she'd refused all of their advances. Now, having reached the ripe old age of twenty-five still bearing her virginity, she thought of it as a stigma.

Evan Hunt, though, affected her in a different way than any man ever had. When she thought of being close to him, lying down with him, taking her clothes off with him, it didn't even seem like a decision, but more a thing that would just simply happen. If he wanted it, that is. And the small squeeze he gave her hand then somehow was enough to say that he did.

Cassie wasn't sure it was the most intelligent move she could make, especially under the circumstances of her dishonesty and the volatility of their very new relationship. And yet she knew...if he touched her, she would touch him back. If he wanted to make love to her, she would welcome it. The thought, the realization, that this long awaited thing could truly finally be only a heartbeat away suddenly made her shiver.

"Cold?" he asked.

"A little," she lied.

"Probably the breeze coming in off the water." He pulled his hand away from hers to slide it around her shoulder, nestling her snugly into the crook of his arm.

"This is nice," she whispered.

She hadn't even realized she'd spoken the words aloud until he replied. "I think so, too."

As warmth flooded her, she became aware of the blood rushing to all the sensitive places in her body. One in particular drew her attention and she released a sigh of want.

And maybe she was crazy, but somehow she thought Evan understood what was happening, and that it was mutual. He stopped walking and turned to face her—then he lifted his hand to cup her cheek. "I know we just met," he told her. "But would you think I was crazy if I said I feel like I've known you a very long time?"

Her lips quivered as her heart pounded violently in her chest. Of course she wouldn't think he was crazy, since she knew exactly what he meant. Even if it all still seemed illogical to her, the rush of emotion overpowered logic. It was as if she'd found the missing piece of herself that she'd always been searching for. Words seemed useless, unnecessary, and impossible, so she simply looked up into his piercing green eyes and shook her head.

She felt wrapped in the warm, sexy scent of him as he slid his arms around her and pulled her close, pressing his chest against her breasts. Were there still other people on the sidewalk? If there were, she couldn't see them. Darkness had fallen quickly and all she could see was Evan's face. His mouth—soft and wanting; his cheeks—rugged with that late day stubble; his eyes—smoldering with heat as they gazed down on her with unbridled passion.

They stood beneath a streetlight and kissed, at first soft and longingly, and then with a fire that both excited and frightened her. She ached for him at the crux of her thighs as his tongue came into her mouth, her lips opening for him. She touched her tongue to his, tentatively at first, but soon reaching and exploring, tasting him, wanting more and more of him.

His hands dropped from her waist to the tight, stretchy material that covered her bottom. He kneaded her firmly there as her hands found their way to his chest, touching him through his shirt, soon clutching at him, bunching the shirt's fabric in her fists. Cassie had never felt so energized and so weakened at the same time. She began to tremble beneath the weight of his kiss, the weight of her desire, the weight of her fear.

And it was a perfectly *valid* fear. Because what if this led where it seemed to be leading? What if she ended up in bed with him? The responses he drew from her came so naturally—the act of sex had never seemed less daunting than in this passionate moment. But what if she slept with him before telling him the truth? And what if, upon finding *out* the truth, he promptly dumped her? Which seemed very likely.

She'd be devastated, that was what. And she hadn't waited all these years just to give her body and soul to a man who would end up breaking her heart.

So she pulled back from him, gasping.

And his eyes shimmered like fiery emeralds on her beneath the streetlights that had illuminated in the falling darkness. "Damn, I'm sorry," he breathed, hands still resting warmly on her hips. "I'm not usually like this. Not usually so pushy."

She swallowed nervously. "Pushy?" The last thing Evan Hunt had been was pushy. Their passion had been entirely mutual.

"I mean, I'm sorry to come on so strong."

"It's all right," she managed to say.

His eyes still bored through her, though, heavy with concern. "I don't want to scare you, Cassandra."

Cassie was fairly horrified by his perceptiveness. "I'm not scared," she claimed. Lying again. But a different type of lie this time. Even if they all funneled back to being about self-preservation.

He tilted his head and spoke softly. "You *look* scared."

"I do?"

He nodded.

She sighed and glanced at her feet, duly embarrassed. "Well, maybe I'm not really used to…you know…being kissed in public…that kind of thing." Cautiously, she raised her eyes to his, struck with a strange sliver of honesty she couldn't hide, and she whispered to him before she could stop herself, "Maybe I *am*...a little scared."

His gaze poured over her, warm and sweet, like liquid heat, drawing her in. "Come here," he said gently, pulling her into a big, comforting hug.

And she murmured, "Thank you," into his chest.

He pulled back just enough to look at her. "For what?"

"Understanding."

And he shook his head easily. "No, thank *you*. For not thinking I'm a jerk." Then he shrugged. "Or at least I *hope* you don't think I'm a jerk."

She smiled. "I know you're not a jerk."

"Listen," he said, grinning softly back at her and taking her hands in his, "until last night I thought I had no room in my life for a woman. Now I'm suddenly feeling like I've got all the time in the world. So we don't have to hurry. We can slow down and take our time. Okay?" Then he lifted her hand to his mouth and placed a silky kiss on her fingers, the sensation threading sweetly outward through her limbs.

As she nodded gently, his suggestion relaxing her fears even if it left her a little physically frustrated, Evan released a soft but sudden laugh.

"What?" she asked, blinking up at him.

"Nothing," he said, shaking his head. "I'm just feeling...you know...like I have a little too much energy right now, and like if I'm going to follow through on this going slow thing, maybe we'd better start running." He ended with a sexy wink.

"Okay," she agreed. Yep, given her own unfulfilled desires, suddenly running didn't sound like such a bad idea. She only hoped Evan wouldn't want to start talking and mess up her concentration again.

She fell in beside him and once more thought she was doing well—until her chest began to hurt and she realized she could barely breathe. But she refused to give in that easily, so she kept running, appreciative of the quiet way Evan slowed his pace for her. The least she could do, she figured, was to keep on trying.

That was when she tripped. Before she knew what was happening, she careened forward toward the sidewalk, instinctively putting out her hands to break her fall before landing with a hard thud. Pain shot through her ankle.

Evan stooped down next to her in an instant, but she couldn't bear to look up and face him. Could she have humiliated herself any worse?

"Are you all right, honey?" he asked. She let out a gasp that nothing to do with her pain and everything to do with what he'd just said. *Honey?* The simple endearment somehow melted her inside, even despite the fall. "Are you okay? Here, let me help you up."

She tried to pull herself together and answer. "I'm fine, except…" She moved a little and—ow! "Except for my ankle."

"Uh-oh," he said, expression grim with concern.

"Here, give me your hands." She did so and tried to stand, but quickly discovered that wasn't going to work. She couldn't put her weight on the ankle, forcing him to slide his arm around her waist and support her until he could lower her onto a nearby bench.

Once there, his arm still around her, he looked into her eyes. "How bad does it hurt? Do we need to get you to the emergency room?"

She shook her head in a rush. "It's just a sprain. What hurts worse," she admitted, "is my pride. I feel like an idiot."

He tilted his head and offered a soft smile. "No need for that. I'm just sorry you're in pain. You sure a quick trip to the ER isn't in order?"

She nodded. She couldn't afford trips to the emergency room. "Positive. It'll feel better after I rest it for a few minutes, I'm sure. Then I'll go home and prop it up on some pillows and it'll be fine."

"Why don't you let me drive you home?" he said. "My car's not far from here. I can run and get it and—"

"Thank you, Evan," she said quickly. "But it's not necessary." She wished she could say yes, but the last thing she needed was to let him see where she lived. No doubt he'd want to come in. Then she'd have to try to explain why she resided in an empty warehouse. No way—she just couldn't deal with that right now.

"Come on, Cassandra," he said. "I can't let you walk on that."

"I'm meeting my friend, Jewel," she lied. "At 8:30.

She wants me to help her…pick out some new workout clothes."

Evan's brow knit. "Don't most of the stores close around that time, if not before?"

"Big sale," Cassie told him. "At an outlet mall. In the suburbs. Someplace Jewel knows about." Where was she getting this stuff?

"Well, you certainly can't shop on that ankle."

"Of course not," she quickly replied. "But I can't just stand Jewel up. Besides, she can take me home and then I can console her on having to miss the sale."

"She wouldn't *miss* the sale if you'd just let *me* take you home," he pointed out.

"But she…can't shop without me," Cassie explained. "She's…um…not very stylish and needs my help." Which, of course, implied that Cassie *was* very stylish, an idea that felt nearly as foreign to hear as going to the Harvard School of Business.

He still looked worried. "Are you sure I can't talk you into letting me drive you? I could take you home, carry you inside, prop up your ankle, and make an ice pack for you. We could order a pizza or something. Doesn't that sound good?"

And she took a deep breath. It sounded *way* more than good. It sounded wonderful. She envisioned the scene: Evan would stay for a while, and maybe after pizza, they'd snuggle while they watched TV and shared a snack. But, she reminded herself again, the couch would sag, the TV only got a few channels, and the only item she had at home that could even remotely be considered snacky was an old box of Pop Tarts.

Evan continued. "We could wait here for Jewel, send her on to the sale, and—"

"Look," Cassie said, feeling adamant, "it's so nice of you to offer, but Jewel can take me home and I'll be fine and that's that. No more arguments. Besides, I get really crabby I get when I'm in pain. See?"

"I don't mind," he persisted.

"Well, I do. Really, I'm just going to go home and go to sleep and I'm sure I'll feel better tomorrow."

Her date let out a sigh, finally defeated. "You make it damn hard for a guy to be heroic."

And she smiled up at him sweetly. "I think you're *very* heroic."

He grinned back, giving her shoulder a soft squeeze. "So, does that mean I can see you tomorrow night?"

My God, this guy really was crazy about her. The knowledge flooded her with renewed joy, even amidst her pain. "Absolutely," she said as a slight warmth bloomed on her cheeks.

"Call me sometime tomorrow at the office to make plans?"

"Sure," she promised. Then remembered her predicament—she had to get hold of Jewel. She started looking around for a phone.

"What's wrong?" Evan asked.

"Um, where are the bathrooms? I need to...go." Dear God, she'd almost said *call Jewel.*

In response, he put his arm around her waist and helped her limp to the park's nearest restrooms. Inside, she found a phone hanging on the wall—hallelujah! But then she realized she had no purse, which also meant she had no quarter. And she certainly couldn't ask Evan for one. She rolled her eyes in despair—this was getting ridiculous.

Desperation grabbed her as a woman appearing to be a fellow runner—and probably far more capable at it—approached to wash her hands. "Excuse me," Cassie said. "I know you don't know me, but I'm badly in need of a quarter. I've sprained my ankle and need to call a friend for help."

The second the woman handed over the coin, Cassie dialed quickly, before anything else could go wrong.

Chapter Six

JEWEL TRIED TO support some of Cassie's weight as she limped down the alley to the warehouse door, but they made slow progress.

"Look," Jewel finally said, "we've got to pick up the pace here. I'm late for my date with Malcolm."

Cassie glanced at her friend, who wore a pair of black boots with pointy toes and high heels. A trench coat covered the rest of her outfit, but Cassie was just as glad—she had a feeling there was leather involved, and probably not much of it. "Besides," Jewel added impatiently, "we're ripe picking for muggers."

Jewel was right. Normally Cassie walked the last couple blocks to the warehouse briskly, trying to exude authority in the hopes of warding off attackers. Tonight, if the muggers were out there, she and Jewel were easy prey. Although the muggers would surely be depressed when they found out she and her friend had nothing to steal.

"Relax," she told Jewel. "I don't think there's a secondary market for sports bras."

"Maybe not. But there *could* be for what *I've* got on."

Cassie couldn't believe the relief she felt at simply reaching her door. Jewel stayed only long enough to get her to the couch, but she didn't mind—she was exhausted and felt like being alone. She propped her leg on throw pillows, supposing that a sensible person would have just let Evan bring her home. A sensible person might even have thought it was a logical time to begin dispelling some of the stories she'd created about herself. But who ever said she was sensible?

She soon regretted her decision. Some help would have been nice. It took an immense effort to move around at all. And as for a shower, that would just have to wait. After a few long minutes of complete boredom and discomfort, she tried to ignore her pain and limped to the kitchen area, which had once served as a break room for warehouse workers. She returned with an ice pack and an ancient Pop Tart. Then she lay down with a sigh and stared at her swollen ankle. This was definitely *not* the life.

Not that it would really take much to make it better. A few days ago, she'd thought it would take a nice apartment, new furniture, a more fashionable wardrobe, and maybe a nice car. At the moment, though, she felt as if the only thing she really needed that she didn't have was Evan. Saggy couch and all, if Evan were there with her, she'd have been happy.

She slept on the couch that night. It wasn't a *good* sleep, but a tossing and turning one. Getting comfortable proved difficult with her ankle propped three pillows high. And when morning finally came, she felt as if she hadn't slept at all.

She glanced up to see that her ankle still appeared somewhat swollen. Not a good sign. Sitting up, she gently lowered her foot to the floor, then slowly attempted to stand. "Ouch," she whispered as she carefully lowered her weight onto it.

Her *ouch* aside, however, turned out it was quite a bit better. But for a girl who worked on her feet all day, *quite a bit better* probably wasn't going to cut it. So she limped to the phone and did something she'd not done even once yet since arriving in Chicago—call in sick. Luckily, Jewel answered.

"Hey, kid, what's up? How's the ankle?"

"Not good."

"Don't tell me. You can't walk."

"I can. Just not very well or for very long."

Jewel sighed and Cassie felt guilty for leaving her friend alone to handle both the breakfast and lunch shifts.

"Sorry about this, Jewel," she said. "Really."

"Don't worry about it," Jewel replied. "I'll call in one of the weekend girls. Get Eddie to pay someone time and a half and they won't mind."

"Eddie will probably have a cow."

"Don't you worry about Eddie, Cass. I'll handle him. Now, you just take care and rest that ankle."

But then something important struck her. "Jewel,

wait. One more thing."

"What?"

"Can you take care of Mac for me today? Four o'clock, by the Dumpster?"

"Sure," Jewel said, and Cassie was thankful to have such a helpful friend.

"And give him something nutritious," she insisted. "What's the soup today?"

"Vegetable."

"Great. That'll be good for him. He'll complain and tell you he doesn't like it and that he'd rather have a cookie or something, but don't let him snow you. He'll eat the soup."

After getting off the phone, Cassie settled back onto on the couch. She supposed she should go back to sleep. She seldom got a chance to sleep in, and she certainly could use some more slumber after her restless night. Still, there was too much on her mind for her to drift off again. If she had a free day, then she would use it to do something productive.

Rising back off the couch, she limped over to her kitchen table to pick up the newspaper she'd gotten from Jewel a couple of days before. And not just to look at the picture of Evan, despite how pleasant a pastime that might be. No, she was going to scour the want ads. She always talked about being a businesswoman, always dreamed of the life she wanted to have. But she'd never taken any real steps to pursue it. At least not yet.

And now's the time. If a miracle occurred and she got

a job quickly enough, maybe it would fill the gaps in some of her lies to Evan, giving some credence to her claims of a job search, and giving her some real knowledge of the business world.

She knew trying to cover her dishonesty that way was horrible, but she found she simply couldn't face the alternative. The longer the charade continued, the more inconceivable it seemed that she could actually admit that she'd lied to him about everything from her name to her education to the town where she grew up. After all, every time she tried, she failed. She knew she'd gotten herself in a ridiculous mess, but she couldn't think of a way out of it besides starting to change some of her lies into truths.

She flipped to the job section in the paper, but once there, she quickly got discouraged. The first job she saw required someone with five years of managerial experience, which was five more than she had. The second wanted a person with a B.A. in business administration, and she figured a potential employer would probably check her credentials a little closer than Evan Hunt had.

Within a few minutes, she found herself dropping the paper on the coffee table in disgust. True, she'd hardly given it a chance, but she just didn't think the job for her was there in black and white. Besides, she didn't even have a resume. Or a business suit for interviewing. And she certainly couldn't afford to go buy one. And Jewel's resourcefulness with clothing could probably only go so far.

Then Cassie's mind drifted back to Princess Cosmetics, to the discussion she'd had with Evan the night before. She started to fantasize about what she'd do for the company if she worked *there*.

She could see herself in a stylish suit and a pair of professional yet slightly sexy heels moving about the office with purpose and authority. And if she had her way, those gaudy old pink tubs and tubes would go. She'd revamp the whole line in favor of something lighter, more modern and inviting, and she'd make them more accessible. She'd...

But wait a minute here. Why was she wasting her time redesigning Princess Cosmetics packaging? Sure, Evan had asked her opinion. But he thought she was a Harvard graduate. In short, he thought she knew what she was talking about, that she was educated, skilled. What good were the opinions of a lowly waitress?

Yet turning back to the want ads was fruitless, too. The first thing her eyes landed on was an ad for a "dancer," which she was pretty sure meant stripper. *No experience necessary. Will train.* She almost wanted to laugh.

And then she started thinking about sex. But not the sordid strip club kind. Instead, she thought of the kind of sex she might have with Evan. It would be beautiful. Absolutely stupendous. All she had ever dreamed.

And there was a big part of her that didn't want to wait any longer, that wanted to drag the man straight to bed. But there was also another part—that frightened part of her which he'd seen so easily—that knew he was right, that they should slow down. She was thankful for his insight and maturity.

Now, if only she could become a businesswoman overnight, one of her major lies could disappear and clear the way for sex without fear of being dumped soon afterward.

EVAN TRIED TO keep his mind on work, but he was secretly waiting for Cassandra to call. Miriam had strict instructions to interrupt him, no matter what he was doing or who was in his office bothering him.

He wanted to find out how her ankle was doing. And he still wished she had let him drive her home and take care of her a little. Nothing against her friend, but he'd just suffered the need to make sure she was all right.

He wondered why she'd insisted on going with Jewel instead of him. *Well, she just met you. Maybe it makes sense, and maybe you were being pushy—just like when you were getting all worked up, making out with her right in the middle of the park—to think she should.* Or...maybe it had been because she was still so nervous around him.

And why *did* she feel so jittery, anyway? The question bothered him.

Did he come off as too powerful, too much the corporate hot shot? Hell, he hoped not. After all, this wasn't exactly a career he'd chosen for himself—it had completely fallen in his lap. And he tried not to let his work make him too money-minded or stuffy.

Lately, of course, he'd had no *choice* but to be money-minded—Princess was on the brink of bankruptcy. But he'd felt a lot more lighthearted since the minute he'd met Cassandra.

He sighed, wishing he'd been able to tell her the whole truth. Besides worrying about her ankle, he'd spent the rest of the night feeling like a piece of shit for fudging the facts on Princess's problems.

Of course, a CEO didn't just go around relaying his company's financial dilemmas to strangers. But she didn't feel like a stranger. And she'd been so concerned and so eager to help out that Evan had ended up feeling like a jerk for just closing down the subject with vague replies.

No wonder she acted nervous. Maybe she could sense my dishonesty.

Thinking of her nervousness again reminded him of the heated kisses they'd shared. She hadn't seemed nervous *then*, not while it was happening. And for a few hot minutes, he could have sworn they were on exactly the same wavelength.

And then she'd suddenly pulled away, shy and sweet and bubbling with an innocence he hadn't seen in a woman in a very long time. Damn if something about it didn't draw him like a moth to a flame.

Though if she *was* innocent, he definitely wanted to be the man to change that.

She'd turned into a completely different person when

they'd started talking about Princess. Her business acumen had shown. Not that she'd said anything highly technical or asked him questions that were difficult by any means, but perhaps that was what he'd found so refreshing about her viewpoint. She'd spoken simply, confidently, and what she'd said had made sense. He'd found himself respecting her opinions and wanting to hear more of them. And not just because he was so taken with her—but because she'd spoken with authority, with the voice of a modern young woman.

That sounded like something Princess Cosmetics could use, in fact. The entire board consisted of men, most of them old ones at that who had been around since his mother's day. Sure, the company employed plenty of females, but they were mostly accountants and administrative people. He couldn't think of one woman who had any input on the creative level.

But—wait, what *creative level?* Creativity at Princess Cosmetics had pretty much died along with his mom.

"Evan," Miriam's voice cut in on his thoughts through the intercom. "Cassandra on line two."

"Great Mir—thanks."

He punched a button and picked up the phone. "Cassandra? Hi. How's your ankle? Better?"

"Well…mostly better."

She'd sounded tentative. "Are you sure? You're not convincing me."

"I'm still limping a little," she confessed. "But it's almost well. Promise."

He sighed, still not sure he believed her. "Well enough that we're still on for tonight? Or—"

"Of course," she cut him off.

And her eagerness to see him anyway made him smile. "Listen," he said, "how about if I pick up some Chinese and just come to your place. We can watch some TV or a movie. That way you can stay off that ankle and let it heal."

On the other end of the phone, however, Cassie frowned. The Chinese sounded fine, but her place definitely did not. Along with the issue of her ancient TV that didn't connect to cable or pick up many channels.

"If you don't mind," she said cautiously, "I'd really rather go out. I've been cooped up here all day resting."

Evan hesitated. "Well, all right," he said. "If you're sure your ankle can take it."

"I am."

"What would you like to do?" he asked.

She hadn't thought of that part. "Hmm, I'm not sure," she mused.

But she immediately wanted to kick herself, sore ankle and all, for not having suggested something. He'd probably suggest some five-star restaurant where she wouldn't be able to read the menu, and in her mind, she was already on the phone to Jewel begging for something appropriate to wear.

"Do you like pizza?" he asked.

"Excuse me?"

"Pizza," he repeated. "Have you ever been to Gino's? Really cool place."

"No," she said, basking in relief. "But it sounds great. Like just what the doctor ordered." Hooray—she could wear blue jeans!

"Good," he said. "And maybe we can catch a movie or something afterwards."

"Sounds fun," she replied.

"Is seven good?"

"Mmm-hmm."

"Where do you live?" he asked.

"Huh?"

"Where do you live? So I can pick you up."

Oh, darn it! And if she offered to meet him someplace again, it would seem weird.

"Cassandra, are you there?"

"Um, yeah, I'm here."

"What's your address?"

Again, she hesitated.

"Come on, Cassandra," he said playfully, "tell me where you live. What's the big deal?"

"Well…the thing is…I don't live in the best neighborhood," she finally admitted. Which was entirely true. And it felt good to finally say *something* true to him.

"So?"

"Well, I…don't want you to get mugged."

But he just laughed. "Don't worry. I'm a big boy."

"Sometimes muggers don't discriminate," she pointed out. "Guns and knives can totally override their fear of big boyness."

"The address?" he insisted again on another chuckle.

She sighed. It was official—she couldn't figure a way out of this one. "2153 Rigby," she said. And then she added the kicker, but it was necessary if he were to find her. "Walk down the alley to the left of the building and ring the bell by the big steel door."

She couldn't believe she'd just handed over her address to him. Especially after all she'd gone through last night to keep it a secret. But it was hard to think fast enough to keep up with this crazy game she'd started. And she supposed it was unrealistic to think she could continue the relationship without him finding out where she lived.

Although it was probably even *more* unrealistic to think she could continue the relationship with these huge lies standing between them, especially considering how they were growing.

And she would have berated herself for the whole thing much longer—but there was simply no time. She had to get ready for her date.

SHE FOUND IT pleasant to dress for a date with Evan on her own, without needing help from Jewel. Still, she wished she had something more fun to wear than what she found in her closet. Her jeans were fine—jeans were like that, shabby ones often looking more stylish than new ones. But her wardrobe of tops and blouses could have used some updating. Finally she settled on a sleeveless pale yellow top she'd owned for years but which flattered her shape and didn't look too worn. Surveying herself in the mirror, she hoped all of her dates with Evan from now on would fall into the blue jeans category.

She brushed her hair and let it fall around her face. Jewel had once told her it looked sexy when she left it down. She added on a pair of simple silver dangly earrings and brown sandals and hoped she didn't look like a total slob.

Just then, she noticed she was walking with relative ease. Her ankle didn't feel perfect, but almost. What a relief. She'd hated the thought of limping through their date—she had enough going against her without adding that impediment to the mix.

When the doorbell sounded, part of her wanted to panic. He was here. And she'd been so consumed with showering and picking out her clothes that the entire afternoon had passed without her manufacturing an explanation for living in a warehouse.

She'd thought about it, of course. She just hadn't come up with anything. And she'd intended to be outside waiting when he arrived and hopefully avoid some of the questions—but she'd lost track of time.

Of course, a normal, sensible person would open the door and let Evan in now. But again, she didn't necessarily fit into that category anymore. So she made him wait while she grabbed her purse and keys, flipped off the lights, and finally slipped out the door into the alley where he stood—without ever letting him get a look inside.

He wore blue jeans even more faded than her own along with a casual shirt and shoes. He looked great, and seeing him dressed just as comfortably as her helped put her at ease.

"Sorry I'm late," he told her. "I almost didn't find this place. You're tucked back in here pretty tightly among all these warehouses. I didn't even realize there were any residences around here."

"Well," she said, "this is…one of those old neighborhoods they're refurbishing." The explanation had popped blessedly into her head in the nick of time.

Though as he looked around, she could almost read his mind. Where on earth was the refurbishment?

"And this is the first place on the list," she added quickly.

He nodded then—and she could see him becoming genuinely interested. "That's cool. What's it like inside?" Ugh. Genuinely interested was not what she needed here.

"Big," she replied simply. "Extremely roomy."

"I bet," he said, leaning back to take in the size of the building. "Is it split up into apartments or…?"

"I'm the only tenant so far," she explained.

And still looking over the exterior, he said, "I'd love to see the inside of the place."

Oh crap. What now? "I'd show you around, but…it's really a mess in there."

"I don't mind," he said with an easy shake of his head. "I'm a guy, after all. We're known for being a little messy sometimes." He ended with a cute laugh.

But this was no time to be swept up into Evan's cuteness—she had to get him out of there. "No, I mean a *big, big* mess. The place is...being remodeled. There are sheets over the furniture. It's awful. In fact," she went on, "the refurbishment I mentioned? It's just being done *now*."

"Wow," he said, blinking. "You must have been anxious to move in."

"Well," she said, "I wanted to be near downtown. And the lake." *And Fast Eddie's.* "So I decided to take what I could get."

Grabbing Evan's hand, she pulled him down the alley toward the street. One more disaster averted.

BY THE TIME they reached Gino's, Cassie had almost managed to forget the new barrage of lies she'd just told.

Evan had held the door of his Saab open for her, a nicer car than she'd ever personally ridden in. The dark interior smelled like leather and masculinity. And as they traveled the Chicago streets, she couldn't deny that it felt a little dreamy to ride in such style.

Evan hadn't been lying—Gino's was a cool place. From top to bottom, the walls, beams, ceilings, and booths were all covered in graffiti left by Gino's patrons over the years. Each table even came complete with a pen to encourage scribbling. The harder part was finding a bare spot on the wall to write your name. Cassie felt extremely at home in her blue jeans.

The two of them shared a large pizza. And she hoped she didn't seem like a pig by eating her full half, but stale Pop Tarts hadn't exactly provided a lot of nourishment over the past twenty-four hours.

Under normal circumstances, she might have felt intimidated by eating something so potentially messy with a classy guy like Evan. But for some reason she felt entirely comfortable—maybe she was finally beginning to just enjoy her time with him without feeling the financial and societal gulfs between them.

And when a chunk of sausage plopped from her pizza back down onto her plate, she started to reach down for it with slightly greasy fingertips—only to see that Evan had beat her to it. She lifted her gaze to meet his—which, to her surprise, had turned suddenly sexy.

Oh my. Was he turned on *now*, right in the middle of pizza?

His eyes said yes. Which, of course, turned her on, too. After all, who could resist that sexy emerald gaze?

That was when he lifted the little bite of sausage to her mouth. And she accepted, parting her lips slightly, using her tongue to remove it from his fingers, which lingered at her lips for a moment afterward.

She had the urge to suck on them, but resisted. The tall wooden booths provided privacy, but not *that much* privacy. So she simply kissed their tips, her eyes locked with his all the while, until finally he pulled his hand away.

He arched one brow and cast a sexy smile across the table, his expression holding just a hint of playfulness. "Not exactly grapes," he said.

"Tasted good to me," she replied from beneath flirtatious lashes.

And she wanted very badly to taste more of him.

Her heart pumped faster at how much she wanted it.

But it seemed too early in the evening to let herself even begin to contemplate such possibilities, so she tried for other conversation. "How was your day?"

He leaned back in his seat and closed his eyes for a second, looking almost as if trying to block out a nightmare—and making her feel bad for bringing it up. "Not so good," he admitted. "Princess stock dropped three points."

"Yikes," she said. She didn't know much about stocks and bonds yet, but the look on his face said it all. "Sorry."

But then he bounced back, giving her a grin. "Which reminds me," he said, "you had the whole day on your hands with nothing to do. Did you think any more about the things we discussed last night?"

Cassie hesitated. She had, of course. In fact, ideas had been popping into her head left and right all day. But what if they sounded stupid? "Yeah," she answered tentatively, "I may have come up with a few thoughts."

"Great." He took a sip from his wineglass. "Let's hear

them."

She tilted her head, still hesitant. "Are you sure?"

"Of course I'm sure."

Okay then. She had no idea how any of this would come across, but if Evan really wanted to know, she would tell him. "Well," she began slowly, "the first thing I would think about is making the products more accessible to the average woman. I'm not suggesting that you market them in drugstores, but have you ever considered selling them outside of the big department stores, maybe stocking them in smaller boutiques where they could be displayed at eye level and women could shop without getting assistance from a salesperson?"

She picked up steam then and started talking faster. "I also think you need to revamp the packaging. I'm sorry to say this, but in my humble opinion, it's just not very attractive. I'm sure it was lovely in your mother's era, but it screams 1960s. And it also screams expensive in an unflattering way. You might consider a more flowery package, something spring-like, more appealing to the eye. Or if you want to retain the pink, maybe go brighter to make it feel more fun and modern, or pull in black and go for a Parisian-feeling motif.

"And another thing, the prices. I know you can't just go lowering all your prices or you'd never make any money, but a lot of women simply can't afford to pay that much. Would you ever consider coming out with more than one line of products, perhaps retaining the current line and adding something more affordable that might appeal to younger women on budgets? So that *every* girl can feel like a princess?"

Cassie stopped, realizing that she'd babbled on for about three times as long as she'd intended before weighing his response. Only now did she dare a look at Evan. And he was smiling. But it was a smile she couldn't quite read.

"I'm sorry. I'm probably way off base here," she volunteered.

But he shook his head and let out a laugh. "Not at all," he said. "I happen to think you're brilliant."

She blinked. Whoa. Had she heard that right? "Brilliant?"

His eyes sparkled on her. "Well," he said with a wink, "if I truly had much business savvy, I guess I wouldn't have to be soliciting suggestions, so who am I to really judge your ideas? But on the other hand, they sound great. Fresh. Innovative. Stylish. Things Princess has been lacking for a while."

She swallowed, still a little taken aback. "So you mean it? You really like my ideas?"

He nodded. "I really do."

And her heart filled with something brand new—a sense of accomplishment and satisfaction she'd never quite experienced. Sure, she'd done fairly well in school, but lack of money and fear of debt had kept her away from higher learning. And she'd always been full of ideas—about everything—but she'd never really had a chance to share them in any meaningful way. So Evan's praise was…beyond validating. She smiled back at him, feeling successful and smart in a way she never had before.

"Of course, I only run the company," he said on another laugh. "That doesn't mean I really make any of the decisions. I'd have to get your ideas past a lot of people before I could put any of them into action. But I think they hold a lot of promise, Cassandra. And that's not something I say lightly."

BY THE TIME they left Gino's, it was almost ten and both agreed it was too late for a movie.

"Want to go for a walk instead?" Evan asked Cassandra, taking her hand once they were out on the sidewalk. "It's a beautiful night. Too soon to go home." Pleasantly warm air surrounded them and a golden moon shone down on the city.

"But wait," he added, suddenly remembering. "That's a bad idea. You need to keep resting that ankle."

"It'll be fine," she insisted. But he'd heard that before and already knew she could sometimes be more optimistic than practical.

Just then, he spotted a horse and carriage up the street, sitting at the curb, waiting for patrons. "I've got a better idea," he said. And with that, he whisked her up into his arms and carried her down the sidewalk toward it.

"Evan," she chided him, laughing as she wrapped one

arm around his neck, "you don't have to carry me. I can walk."

"No," he said teasingly, "I don't trust you to take care of yourself. So I'm going to have to do it for you. You're not taking any unnecessary steps until we get home, young lady, and that's that."

Cassandra smiled sweetly up at him and he couldn't wait to get her alone in the carriage. Normally the romantic look in her eyes might worry him a little. But then, normally he wasn't one to take women on carriage rides, either. Normally he would worry that such a romantic act would make a woman take the relationship too seriously, make her want more from him than he wanted to give. But nothing with Cassandra was normal. With her, he suffered none of that regular hesitance. With her, he felt only a sense of connection—and a growing passion.

Once he'd lifted her up into the white carriage and paid the elderly driver to show them the city, still more inspiration struck. "Wait," he told the old man. Then he jogged a few steps further up the sidewalk and bought a red rose from a street vendor.

And hell, maybe this was corny; maybe he was going overboard and would end up feeling silly—but he found himself wanting to do everything right with her, make everything perfect. He might be withholding the truth about his business, but he promised himself that would be the *only* error he'd commit in their relationship. And he'd correct that one soon—he really would.

He still couldn't explain the change that had come over him since he'd met her a mere two nights ago, but he'd surrendered to it all the moment he'd taken her in his arms on the dance floor.

When he offered the rose to Cassandra, her eyes lit up. Lowering himself into the seat next to her, he slid his arm around her shoulder and pulled her close against him. Then he reached into the floor of the carriage and drew a woven blanket up over their laps. It wasn't cold out, but Evan had the urge to be under covers with her.

The driver led the horse and carriage away from the curb with a slow clopping of hooves and the city street began to creep past them, the surrounding skyscrapers and sidewalks—usually so intrusive and busy—seeming suddenly serene.

"This is perfect, Evan," she whispered up into his ear.

Her breath felt warm there—just before she lowered her head to rest it on his shoulder.

When the pressure of her breast came snug at his side and her thigh pressed against his beneath the blanket they shared, he knew she was right. This was perfect. And he couldn't keep from kissing her a minute longer.

Chapter Seven

MOVING HIS HAND under the blanket, Evan reached to lift her legs over his so that he could better take her into his arms. Then his mouth found hers.

He kissed her soft lips—slow, warm, tender—but soon let his mouth trail downward. The gentle fluttering of her breath wafted up into the night as she leaned her head to one side, offering her slender neck up for more kisses. The tiny effort on her part—what struck him as almost an instinctual invitation—fueled his desire. She wanted him there, welcomed his affections.

With one hand in her flaxen hair, the other gripping her hip, he brought his mouth to her earlobe. The tiny earring she wore touched his tongue and he licked a small circle around it. Her breath grew audible, quivery, and—damn, he needed more of her.

He slid his hand gingerly from her hip upward to her breast, at first gently cupping the side, then taking it full into his hand. She felt exquisite in his grasp, her taut nipple grazing his palm through her top and bra, and Evan suddenly wished they weren't in a carriage. He wished they were alone, in a bed. He wanted desperately to be inside her. He wanted to make her feel everything that was warm and wild and good. He wanted to drown her inhibitions in his passion.

As if the thought were a bad omen, though, she gasped slightly then and pulled away from him. And he peered into her eyes, fearing the alarm he would see there.

Only instead…he saw something less, and also something more. The alarm he'd expected actually looked more like just a hint of hesitation, of realization, realization of what was happening between them, what was building here—and mixed into her gaze with those things was the same hunger as his own. It added to the arousal that already had him hard and wanting.

He offered a tentative grin. "Going slow with you isn't as easy as I thought," he whispered, "but I'm going to keep trying."

Her gentle smile was almost inviting—she teased him with a flirtatious little bite on her lower lip. "I'll forgive you if you slip up every now and then."

He tried to calm the fury inside him, tried not to let the nearly overpowering heat he suffered leak from his eyes—but he knew he failed.

Then again, if Cassandra's fear was beginning to dissipate, maybe his hunger for her was okay. Maybe she would even welcome it. Maybe soon she'd let him get closer. Maybe soon.

EVAN GENTLY EASED Cassie back against the metal door
that led to her warehouse home. Her body tingled with
wanting him—her breasts yearned for more of his touch,
and the sensations between her thighs begged her to
loosen up and let herself have the man. God knew she
wanted to.

But she was afraid. For more reasons than one.

Although she knew fear could only hold her body at
bay for so long.

His kisses snaked through her limbs, the pleasure it
delivered reaching even her fingertips and toes. A tender
ache of desire gripped the small of her back and she
pulled in her breath in an attempt to quell it.

"I had an amazing time tonight," he rasped in her
ear, voice low and sexy.

"Me too," she whispered back.

Then his mouth came down on hers again, kissing
her harder this time, making her feel ready to surrender—to everything with him. His hands molded to her
bottom, kneading her roughly, rhythmically, amplifying
the intense pulsing between her legs.

She returned his kisses hotly, eagerly, her body more
in control than her mind for a change, and she wondered
if he would soon be expecting her to ask him inside. Of
course, that didn't matter. Even if she wanted to, she
couldn't.

Finally, *he* asked *her* instead. "Don't suppose I could

get you to invite me in?" Longing filled his playful gaze, and the same heady desire flowed through her veins, as well.

"I…I can't," she breathed. Oh God—it felt strange and horrible to tell him no, especially when it was so clear that they both wanted each other.

"Why not?" he asked softly. "You don't want to?"

She shook her head. "No, it's not that. It's…it's…the remodeling. Remember, I told you what a mess it is in there. An absolute pigsty. I can barely stand to be there myself."

His eyebrows shot up. "It's that bad?"

She nodded profusely, praying he believed her.

And in response, he thoughtfully tilted his head to one side—then said the impossible, as if it were the most normal thing in the world. "If it's that awful, why don't you come stay with me for a while?"

"Wh-wh-what?" she sputtered.

"I know it sounds crazy, and that we haven't known each other long," he said, "but I won't make any assumptions, I promise. I'll sleep on the couch if you want. But there's no good reason for you to stay here in a construction zone when I have a big condo all to myself. And besides," he added tentatively, "if I'm being totally honest here, I guess I…just don't want to say goodnight."

Well, at least one of them was being honest here—and as a result, Cassie feared her heart would leap from her chest. She sighed, then took one look into Evan's inviting green eyes, the eyes that had captured her heart the very first moment they met, and knew she couldn't turn them down. "If…if you're sure…"

"I am," he quickly assured her. "It'll be like…a slumber party." Then he winked. "Between grown-ups. Of the opposite sex. Who like each other a lot." Only then he looked a little worried about what he'd just said. He help up his hands in defense. "But I promise—no assumptions, really. I'm truly fine on the couch."

She let a tentative smile take shape on her face. Then she bit her lip thoughtfully, letting go of a last bit of hesitation, and said, "All right. Just give me a few minutes to throw some stuff in a bag."

"Great," he said.

Then she unlocked her door and stepped quickly inside, shutting Evan out in the alley. Despite knowing that he surely stood out there thinking her a total weirdo for not letting him come inside while she packed, she basked in relief. Because once she went to his place, she wouldn't have to deal with this dilemma again. At least for a while.

She pulled her old suitcase out from under her bed and opened it up. After grabbing some more blue jeans and tops, underwear and bras, she tossed them all inside, then gathered toiletries from the bathroom—which, like the kitchen, had already existed in the warehouse, complete with a shower stall.

Then she thought of tomorrow, and of Fast Eddie's Diner. Of course, she could just shuck the job and hope

Evan meant to take care of her for the rest of her life, but that was more than just a little unrealistic. And as wonderful and rich as Evan was, she wasn't sure she wanted to be taken care of in that way. So she located the two pink uniforms she rotated, grabbed her nametag from the dresser, and stuffed the whole handful in the bottom of the suitcase beneath everything else.

Only that was when she thought of another reality she'd have to deal with. Getting up at five AM and rushing out the door. Nobody gave job interviews that early. So she next found some workout clothes Jewel had left at her apartment the other night and packed those, too. She would have to add an additional lie to her repertoire and claim early morning classes at some gym she didn't really belong to.

As she shut the suitcase, Cassie couldn't believe she was really doing this. But *she* didn't want to say goodbye to Evan, either. And the idea of being so close to him was an invitation she simply couldn't resist.

THE LONG ELEVATOR ride up to Evan's place made Cassie anticipate something plush and breathtaking. When they entered through large double doors and he flipped on a lamp, the low lighting and dark masculine decor didn't allow her to see much, but she knew her instincts had been correct. Expensive-looking furniture dotted the spacious condo and serious-looking pieces of art decorated the walls. She took a deep breath. She had entered Evan's world.

After carrying her suitcase to the bedroom, he returned to the living room where he'd left her enjoying the view—though now she'd stepped through a set of French doors led to a balcony that seemed to overlook all of Chicago. The lights below struck Cassie as a mirror reflection of the sky, like a valley of stars.

As he joined her, she said, "Pretty view."

"Better when you have someone to share it with," he told her, wrapping his arms around her from behind.

She shuddered at his touch, feeling unreasonably warm inside—and Evan backed off, which both relieved and disappointed her.

"Sorry," he told her, smiling sheepishly. Like other times when he'd let her see certain vulnerabilities, the expression was oddly endearing on such a strong man. "I already forgot my promise. No expectations or assumptions."

"Evan, thank you. For letting me stay here. And also for…being so understanding. About going slow. Not every guy would be."

"I should be the one thanking *you*. Because I know this is awfully damn fast to be doing something like this—inviting you to stay with me. But I'm really happy you're here." His smile ignited a slow burn inside her.

She met his gaze and returned it. "Me, too."

And when next she looked up into his wanting eyes, she knew it pretty much came down to having sex or saying goodnight.

"Well...I guess I should get some sleep," she told him, half regretting the decision already but knowing it was probably wise. They weren't going slow at anything else—this should be the one thing she took her time at.

He nodded in understanding. "The bathroom is right off the bedroom," he told her. "Towels are in the corner cabinet."

"Thanks."

And with that, she headed straight for the bedroom without even so much as a kiss, suddenly anxious to escape before temptation lured her.

Large and equally as masculine as the rest of the apartment, Evan's room provided her with needed sanctuary. Now that she was really here, it felt strange and uncomfortable to be in such foreign surroundings, but she tried to settle in and feel at home. And only when she popped open her suitcase did she realize—in her rush to leave the warehouse, she'd forgotten to pack pajamas.

Oh boy.

She considered her options.

She could sleep nude. But no way—bad idea. Evan was right in the next room and anything could happen without a clothing barrier of some kind.

She could paw through his drawers on her own and find something to wear. But that seemed so invasive. And as much as one part of her would have loved to go digging through his drawers and into his life, she didn't want to violate his privacy that way.

Or...she could go ask him for something to wear. It seemed like the only sensible answer.

Feeling extremely childish having forgotten something so key, she padded back out into the living room where he still stood peering out the French doors. "Evan?" she whispered.

He looked up, then smiled. "Yeah?"

"Um, this is embarrassing," she began, "but...I forgot to bring any pajamas. Could you, um, possibly lend me something to sleep in? A T-shirt or something?"

His look became a mixture of amusement and disappointment and she knew he'd hoped her return had meant something else, something more. Still, he said, "Sure. Follow me," and headed toward the bedroom she'd just departed.

Once there, he opened a dresser drawer and pulled out a large gray T-shirt with the words *Northwestern University* emblazoned in maroon. "How's this?"

"Perfect," she said, taking it from his hand. Their fingertips brushed slightly, enough to send a mild tremor through her body.

He headed to the doorway, but then stopped to peer back at her, the wistful, wanting look in his eyes almost making something inside her hurt. "Goodnight," he said.

"Goodnight, Evan."

She watched him disappear, but he stuck his head back in the door only a second later. "And Cassandra?"

"Yes?"

"I meant what I said before. I'm glad you're here.

Even with the going slow part."

She smiled and watched as he closed the door behind him. And she let her eyes rest there for a moment, but this time he didn't return.

She sighed at his departure, wishing she could control all the confusing feelings inside her. These decisions about sex were difficult enough without her having thrown a bunch of lies into the mix. Why, oh why, had she ever lied to him in the first place? And how, oh how, had she gotten herself into this spot—into his home, and even into his *bed*, for heaven's sake?

Entering Evan's bathroom revealed that, as bathrooms went, his wasn't unusual. Dark towels hung neatly on towel bars, and only one cascaded haphazardly over the shower door. She supposed it might have been from earlier, from getting ready for their date.

And she tried not to picture him *in* the shower—she really did—but the beautiful vision snuck into her mind anyway, and she had to grip the sinktop for a second and catch her breath.

She fought the temptation, the same as with his drawers, to open his medicine cabinet or look beneath his sink. What kind of soap did he use? What kind of toothpaste? Deodorant? What else might she find? She simply wanted to hold onto him, to all the tiny pieces that made him. She wanted to touch the things he touched every morning, wanted to be closer to him in any tiny way she could.

You could just go lie down with him on the couch if you

want to be so close to him.

After washing her face, she used the towel tossed over the shower door rather than the one Evan had laid out for her. That was as close as she could let herself get to him for the moment.

Pulling the Northwestern T-shirt over her head, she turned back the covers on his large sleigh bed. Then she slid beneath the dark gray sheets and tugged the coordinating comforter over her. Simple and masculine, same as in the bathroom.

Was it feeling the sheets he slept on or being in the T-shirt he'd worn that had such a strong effect on her as she tried to go to sleep? She could smell him. All around her. She could even almost feel him, too. Pleasant sensations, but they made her restless. She tossed and turned, each movement seeming to stir up scents of him more. Finally, she held herself very still, trying to kill the sensation of him, trying to make it all go away.

Reaching up to touch her breasts through the T-shirt, she found that her nipples had hardened and turned suddenly sensitive. She crossed her legs tightly, one over the other, trying to blot out the feelings that quivered—actually almost sizzled—between them.

She stayed in the big bed trying to relax and be sleepy, trying to think of anything else but Evan Hunt. But his possessions were all around her, his life and his aura practically cocooned her, and his hot, sexy body lay right in the next room. She knew she'd never be able to sleep.

What she *didn't* know was what exactly she was planning to do when she left the bed and walked out into the living room—only that her feet led her there.

Evan lay on the couch covered with a sheet, his chest bare and sexy, his dark hair mussed.

"Evan?" she whispered.

He opened his eyes and focused on her standing at the foot of the sofa.

"I'm sorry, but…this isn't going to work," she said.

"What isn't going to work?"

"It would seem that…well—that I can't be this close to you and go to sleep."

He smiled softly at her through the darkness. "And what do you suggest we do about it?"

She took a deep breath. "I was thinking that…maybe you could…come in the bedroom and lie down with me."

"Cassandra," he began, his tone one of reasoning, "if going to sleep is really what you want to do, lying down together might just make it a hell of a lot more difficult."

Cassie didn't know what to say. Her lips trembled and she wondered if he could see that in the darkened room. She couldn't even explain to *herself* what she was feeling, let alone to him—but she simply couldn't bear to return to his big warm bed alone. "But I want…I want…"

"What, honey?"

She bit her lip. "I don't know."

Evan pushed the sheet aside and stood from the

couch. He wore gray boxer briefs and nothing else. Even in the half light of the room, she could see through the underwear that he was hard, the sight at once arousing yet making her feel wary.

He came toward her and wrapped his arms warmly around her. And as his hardness pressing against her abdomen, it again heightened both her desire and also her fear. "Cassandra, sweetheart," he began. "Whatever you want me to do, I will. I just want to make you happy. I want to give you whatever you need. But you have to help me. You have to tell me."

Cassie shuddered in his arms as she lifted her eyes to his. This was all up to her. Right now. In this moment. "I...I want you," she said.

Evan's gaze turned sexy. "I want you, too, honey. More than I can say."

"But...the truth is that...I'm afraid, Evan."

He held her closer and rubbed her back. "What are you afraid of?" he murmured, voice low and comforting.

"I...I..."

He pulled back to look at her. "What is it, baby?"

She shook her head and swallowed in a big gulp, embarrassed. She felt so immature, like a little girl who'd been masquerading as a grown-up.

"I don't mean to pry," he prodded her. "I just want to understand."

"Well..." What would he think when he found out the woman he thought so worldly was a virgin. But she knew she wanted to love him, wanted to take him inside her, wanted to give herself to him, and she knew with near-certainty that it was going to happen *now*. And so she knew she had to tell him, knew she *had* to be honest with him about *this*. "Well, the thing is, I'm nervous because I haven't ever exactly...done this...before."

"Haven't ever exactly done *what* before?"

She let out a sigh, trying to find the words. Given her age, it felt hard to say, hard to admit. "You know. I'm a...a..."

That was when he curled his hands onto her shoulders as he looked into her eyes with near understanding. "Cassandra, are you trying to tell me that...you're a virgin?" He'd whispered the word.

And she simply nodded.

"Oh honey," he said, pulling her close, making her feel warm and safe and perfect. Then he gazed down at her again. "But why?" he asked. "Why haven't you ever..."

Another sigh crept out. "Well, I just never found anyone who...who I felt that strongly about. Back in high school, Jimmy Hickson really loved me, but I didn't feel the same. Since him, the only guys I've ever really gotten close to seemed like they were *only* interested in sex and that turned me off. I guess the real answer is that, well, I never...fell in love with anybody before."

Evan's eyes looked amazing, like she'd just offered him a gift. "Do you think you might love *me*?" he whispered cautiously.

"Yes." Finally, some truth between them. And that

one word spilled from her lips more easily than any other she'd said to him in quite a while.

Evan released a deep, guttural sigh that made her want him all the more madly. "I'm falling in love with you, too, Cassandra. And I'd have told you sooner, but…I just didn't want to scare you."

Cassie's heart beat wildly, hearing those words. And then she explained, "It's not love I'm scared of. Really, it's not. It's the other part. The thing that comes with it…" She stopped and sighed, frustrated with herself.

Yet Evan's sweet smile engulfed her. "I don't want you to be afraid, honey. I just want to love you. I want to show you how good it can be."

She peered up at him, speechless, taking in his words, wondering if it could be that easy.

"No reason to be nervous," he promised her softly. "I'll take my time, be slow and easy about it. I'll make it so good for you, honey—I swear. I'll make it what you want it to be."

Cassie drew in her breath at the realization of how close it all lay—as Evan added, "If…that's what you want."

And then she knew. Finally, with no more worry, no more doubt—only trust.

"Yes," she said. "That's absolutely and totally what I want. And I want it right now."

Chapter Eight

───────❦───────

T HE MOMENT WHEN Evan whisked Cassie up into his arms and carried her into the bedroom felt no less than surreal. After he laid her tenderly on the dark sheets, she looked up to see his body silhouetted against the window behind him. Her heart beat fast and furious in her chest, and in one way she hated herself—for waiting this horribly long in life, for making this moment so intimidating instead of joyful. Yet in another way she was *glad* she'd waited—she knew it was right, she knew *this moment* was right, she knew *Evan* was right—and the realization flooded her with the joy she'd been missing.

When he lay down and reached out to touch her arm, she shivered and drew in her breath. Clearly sensing her apprehensions, he reached down for her hand and gently brought it to his mouth. He placed tiny kisses on each of her fingers, then dropped even more raindrop-like kisses to the soft valleys where her fingers met her hand. Soon his mouth journeyed slowly up her arm, bestowing still more sweet kisses, one particularly memorable one on the soft skin of her inner elbow that caused a blissful sigh.

As his kisses trailed over her shoulder and onto her neck, she finally began to forget herself, forget her fears. Each touch of his lips to her body felt like a tiny piece of heaven.

"Oh Evan," she breathed as he rolled to cover her body with his, soon kissing her closed eyelids, her forehead, her cheeks. His hard, solid form pressed warmly into each curve and rise of her own, but his kisses stayed soft and undeniably potent. She'd never realized that hard and soft could complement each other so perfectly.

When he deposited a tiny kiss on the tip of her nose, it tickled and a light giggle escaped her. She opened her eyes to see him smiling playfully down at her. "Am I doing okay so far?" he asked.

She gave him a delicate smile, along with a nod. He was doing perfect.

When Evan finally lowered his mouth to hers, she let her head sink deep into the pillow as she absorbed the sensations arcing through her body. Desire cocooned her and she didn't flinch when his hands slid gently from her waist to her breasts. She simply sighed her pleasure at his touch and absorbed his wonderful affections.

"It still sounds a little crazy to say this so soon, I know," Evan whispered close to her ear, "but I love you."

She breathed the same sentiment back at him, consumed with his hands and his mouth and the way he used them to excite and soothe her all at the same time.

When he began to lift her T-shirt over her head, she didn't object—she let it happen. She'd feared this moment—feared she would feel on display or scrutinized somehow. But instead, all she felt was love. And like everything about the moment was meant to be. She knew she belonged there—in his bed, in his arms, beneath his eyes.

Fire raced through Cassie's veins when flesh met flesh, when Evan's hands found her bare breasts. He molded tenderly, stroking her beaded nipples with his thumbs.

She gasped when he took one sensitive peak into his mouth, licking at it provocatively—and couldn't hold in her moans as the thick sensations coursed through her. He lifted his head only long enough to meet her gaze with his own before bestowing the same delectable treatment upon the other breast. And then he rasped her name against her soft flesh. "Mmm, Cassandra."

Of course, that wasn't really her name, and the sound of it being whispered so lovingly from Evan's lips stuck in her mind even as she basked in the pleasure he gave her. *Cassandra*. It sounded wrong—it wasn't her.

But it was her right now. It *had* to be. She had to believe she was truly Cassandra.

And there was something about that thought that actually...made her body grow suddenly impatient. In so many ways, Cassie felt like a little girl compared to Evan—but Cassandra...Cassandra was more of a woman. She was more educated. More confident. She knew what she wanted out of life and had a plan to get it. And…even if she was a virgin, maybe Cassandra wasn't quite as afraid of sex as Cassie was.

Her breathing turned to panting and she clutched at him, at his neck and broad shoulders, at the muscles in his arms. She clawed her fingers desperately through his hair. He drew on her breast with his mouth until she thought she might explode. And all the while she became more and more keenly aware of the rock hardness that pushed against her inner thigh. She wanted more of it. And she wanted it higher up, between her legs.

And he seemed to read her mind, because that was when his touch came there, his fingers sinking there, where she ached for him. She gasped at the rush of pleasure, let her legs instinctively spread.

And as he began to touch her that way, rubbing small, tight circles with his skilled fingertips, low moans began to escape her. She bit her lip as her eyes fell shut. His touch, there, was enough for a girl to get lost in—enough to make her forget any other aspect of life existed.

Jimmy Hickson had touched her this way on a few occasions. But it hadn't felt like *this*. It hadn't made her move instinctively against his hand this way. It hadn't utterly consumed her this way. It hadn't made her forget her shyness or inhibitions this way.

High whimpering sounds she'd never heard from herself before began to echo from her throat as she felt herself nearing a certain peak, striving for a certain completion.

And then—oh—it happened. Supreme pleasure burst forth from that one little spot where he touched her, making her cry out, clutch helplessly at him, want to cling to him, as her whole body vibrated from it for a few hot, glorious seconds that were quite possibly the best of her life so far.

"Oh baby," Evan murmured. "So sweet." He kissed her on the forehead.

And she nuzzled against him and nearly purred, "Oh my God—that was amazing."

She took in his heated smile, the sultry sexual glint in his eye. And then she longed desperately for more of him—in a whole new way. "Please," she heard herself whisper desperately.

He pulled back to look into her eyes and his voice came out raspy. "Please what, honey?"

Her lips trembled. "I want to know what you feel like...inside me."

He swallowed visibly, his eyes glossing over with a new level of passion. "Oh honey," he breathed, burying his head in the curve of her neck. "I want that, too."

"I can't wait anymore, Evan," she said. "I need to feel this, to have this."

His breath sounded ragged above her as he raised his body enough to slip his fingers into the waistband of her cotton panties and pull them to her ankles and off.

Kneeling before her, he removed his boxer briefs and Cassie saw his body in shadow—and even in the darkness, she could somehow *feel* their new nakedness, the lack of any barrier between them.

She watched as he reached over to the night stand. Heard the opening and shutting of a drawer. Paper tearing. His labored breath above her.

"Wh-what are you doing?" she finally whispered.

"Protection," he replied.

"Of course," she said, feeling stupid.

Silence seemed to hang in the dark air for a long moment until he asked her in a sexy whisper, "Are you ready, honey?"

Cassie took a deep breath. "Yes."

She heard her own rough gasps as Evan's warm hands gently pushed her legs apart. It shocked her to see his head dip swiftly down between them, though, and she cried out with an unexpected jolt of intense pleasure when his tongue took one long stroke up her middle, seeming to slice into her core.

He quickly kissed her stomach. And the valley between her breasts.

His face hovered above hers as he gripped her hips and she felt him pushing at the cleft between her legs. "This may hurt a little," he warned.

She tensed. "I know."

And then it came, the sudden entry, both forced and welcome, and a low groan pushed through her clenched teeth.

"Are you all right?"

She tried to calm her breathing. "I think so."

She lay beneath him, feeling him inside her, slowly beginning to move in her, slowly beginning to love her with his body. At first she held very still, trying to adjust to the sensation, getting used to it, coming to know it. Soon, though, she wrapped her arms around his neck and held to him tightly, beginning to relax, beginning to like this, beginning to want this and to move softly against his tender thrusts.

"Oh God, Cassandra," he moaned above her.

She held him even tighter, wanting their bodies to become one, wanting to own him somehow, possess him. Tears formed in her eyes, but they weren't from fear or pain or anything bad. They came from the intense connection of their bodies, the connection of their hearts. As those tears began to trickle down her cheeks, Cassie felt more complete and alive than ever before.

His cheek brushed against hers. "Are you crying?" he whispered.

"Yes." But eager to quell his fears, she added, "Because I'm happy."

Evan's grip on her grew stronger then, his movements becoming harder and faster as she closed her eyes and saw colors she'd never known before. "Oh God, Cassandra," he said again, panting and heaving. "Oh God."

Soon he collapsed, spent and heavy, against her body. And when Cassie opened her eyes, his face lay only inches away. "You're beautiful," he told her. "Do you know that?"

Only now that it was over and she could think again, her tremors returned, even if only slightly. "Did I...do okay?"

He laughed. "Honey, you did beautiful, I promise."

She bit her lip. "Thank you," she told him. "For making this so wonderful."

"This is just the beginning," he said.

Cassie curled her body against his, resting her head in the crook of his neck. She thought she was going to like this being in love stuff.

WHEN CASSIE OPENED her eyes, the first thing she saw was Evan's chest, broad and muscular and dusted with dark hair. She wanted to touch it, kiss it. But she didn't want to wake him. One glance at the clock on the night table told her that if she hurried, she might not be late for work. She felt thankful the first hints of daylight had awakened her.

Still, it was difficult to pull away from him, hard to leave the feel and scent of him behind. Sleeping with him, their bodies touching, had given her the sense of being connected to him, and when she eased away from him across the sheets, she felt the loss.

She lay still for a moment, watching him breathe, eyes closed, his delicate lashes seeming out of place and yet somehow perfect against his strong face. He needed to shave. But she wished he wouldn't. He looked rugged and perfect and she wished it would never change, that the moment would never end.

She groaned inside as she forced herself to slip out of bed, the act reminding her of her own nakedness. How strange to wake up like that, her bare body pressed up against another bare body. A *hard, beautiful* bare body. How delicious it felt.

She padded to the bathroom with a smile on her face. Glad the mystery of sex was finally over. Glad she'd waited for the right man. And Evan was indeed the right man. The perfect man. She only wished that *she* could be as perfect as she'd led him to believe.

Closing the bathroom door, she stepped into the shower—and she tried to rush but found it difficult. Evan's shampoo was in there. And his soap, masculine in scent and beige in color. She rubbed it over her skin thinking how it had also been rubbed over *his*. She'd thought perhaps making love to him would squelch her fascination with all the items that were him, but instead it had only intensified her curiosity, her need to touch and feel and understand everything about him.

By the time she exited the shower, she knew she would be late. But darn it, Eddie would just have to understand. She'd just had the most important, most precious night of her life. Not that she was going to go into that with Eddie. To him, she'd have to pretend that her ankle was still slowing her down.

She reached again for the towel Evan had tossed over the shower door last night. She didn't want a clean, fresh-smelling towel—she wanted a musky, Evan-scented towel. She folded it around herself and drank in his shower-fresh scent.

Okay, you're seriously wrapped up in the guy, but it's time to get back to reality. There were tables to wait on, and lies to maintain. She sighed heavily. And still no answer to her predicament on the horizon.

In case Evan woke up as she was leaving, she slipped into a pair of leggings and a zip-up hoodie, ready to claim it was workout time. She moved quietly into his kitchen and rifled through the pantry until she found a shopping bag, in which she packed her waitress uniform along with a pair of jeans and a casual top to wear home. She wrote him a note explaining her absence, her heart beating hard and painful with the extension of the many lies she'd told him.

Yes, being in love was wonderful, but that didn't mean it was easy. The closer she grew to him, the harder living a lie became.

EVAN FELT THE sun on his face, but didn't open his eyes. He decided to allow himself some luxuries today—the ease of waking up slowly, the convenience of being the boss and going in late. Miriam would worry, but not much. She'd known he had a "hot date," as she'd called it. His absence this morning would merely confirm her suspicions of just how hot it had been.

He smiled in his half-awake state; hot was certainly one way to describe it. Hot, and yet somehow amazingly soft at the same time. Before last night he'd not realized anything so soft could be that totally heated, but going to bed with Cassandra had taken him to a new place. Her body had been all he'd imagined and more. Her creamy breasts, so sensitive to his touches and kisses, and all the curves below, so pristine and untouched. But he stopped then, amending that thought. They'd been untouched *before last night*. He shuddered at the memory.

He didn't think he'd ever touched a woman so gently before. In fact, he hadn't even known he had it in him—but she'd inspired an immense tenderness. Perhaps it had been finding out that she was giving him the gift of herself for the first time. Or maybe it was simply being in love.

It had surprised him to discover that a girl so lovely and sweet had gone this long in life without sharing her body with anyone. But then again, maybe it *wasn't* such a shock. Maybe deep down he'd sensed it—maybe it had been apparent in her nervousness when they were close and in the shy way she'd reacted to his advances. Maybe he'd been surprised...*not* to find out that she was a virgin, but that of all the guys in the world, she wanted him to be *the one*.

Aw, to hell with waking up slowly—he wanted to see Cassandra, her pretty blond hair spread on the pillow next to him, her beautiful face so alive with sweetness. He opened his eyes and rolled toward her.

But he found only an unfluffed pillow and wrinkled sheets.

His heart sank. *I didn't dream her, did I?*

No—being inside her sweet body had been far too real to be imagined, far too incredible.

Still, she seemed like the last girl who would cut and run. Unless…she was sorry they'd had sex. Damn. He swallowed, stung by the possibility that she'd decided sleeping with him was a mistake.

He rolled over on his back, hands behind his head, contemplating the idea—and sulking about it. He sighed, then shifted his gaze to steal a glance at the clock. 8:15. And then he noticed a sheet of paper from the note pad he kept by the bed. He snatched it from the night table.

Evan, I had an early class at the gym and didn't want to wake you. Please leave a key for me with the doorman. Last night was beyond perfect. See you tonight. C

Oh. Okay. Good. He could breathe again.

And then he even smiled. She would see him tonight. He liked the idea of that, of coming home to her. It was no fun waking up without her, but being able to look forward to seeing her again made it all worthwhile.

Besides, today was Friday. One more day at the office and then he had the whole weekend to spend with Cassandra.

CASSIE SLID THE key into the lock and pushed open the door. Quiet filled the condo. Evan wasn't home.

Walking in, she breathed a sigh of relief and let herself sink into the deep leather sofa. She'd been unsure how she was going to explain her attire if he were here. Jeans and a T-shirt were not exactly interview clothes. Well, not unless you wanted to work at a convenient store—or wait tables at Fast Eddie's Diner.

She had concocted a lie should she need it, though. She'd been prepared to tell him she'd spent the afternoon at the library doing job research. But her pulse raced still. Due to the lie itself. Due to *all* the lies. The whole horrible predicament had grated on her mind all day— she'd even messed up customers' orders and recited specials from last week.

What kind of person am *I?*

She tried to think she was a *good* person, a *kind* one. She cared about people, right? Mac, for example. In fact, she cared a great deal about *all* the people she'd come to know at the shelter.

But was caring enough? Could all the rights in a person's life make up for a colossal wrong like lying to the man you loved?

And making love to Evan had just made everything worse.

Okay—well, not *everything*. Physically, she felt fabulous. And ready for more.

But now, every time her dishonesty so much as crossed her mind, her stomach twisted with an even deeper guilt than before.

For the first time since coming to Evan's place last night, she got a good look at it. Her initial impression still held—luxurious, rich, and manly. Brown leather furniture set amid sleek, modern side pieces. The latest technology graced the room as well. And the books in the dark pine case against the wall were mostly business-related—Cassie couldn't find one novel among them.

Yet despite feeling a little intimidated by the atmosphere, nothing about it was...bad. No, it was just Evan. Sitting in the room was like sitting inside him. And realizing that he'd probably selected everything here himself, Cassie started having that feeling again—that when she touched his things, she touched *him*. She put her hands on the leather of the sofa to each side of her, finding it cool to the touch.

Thinking about the masculinity of the place, about *Evan's* masculinity, spurred her heart to beat faster. Settling deeper into the big sofa, she tried very hard to think of other things.

She considered getting more acquainted with the kitchen and trying to prepare Evan a nice dinner, but she was really a better waitress than a cook. Besides, she had no idea when he'd be home—it could be hours.

So she meandered into the bedroom with the intent of looking out the window, seeing a different view than the one provided by the French doors in the living room—but instead her gaze was drawn to the big sleigh bed she'd shared with Even just last night. When he'd made love to her. Taken her virginity. And suddenly she couldn't wait until he got home so they could do it again.

Feeling playful and a little daring, Cassie contemplated how she could surprise him when he came home. Going into the bathroom, she brushed her hair, letting it fall about her shoulders. Then, without weighing the idea much, she took off her T-shirt and shed her bra along with it. She kicked off her shoes, then stripped off her jeans and panties, as well.

Should she climb into bed and wait for him? Or just help herself to a robe and lounge in front of the TV, acting as if she always came home and slipped into next to nothing? Of course, she had no robe and the big terrycloth one that hung on the back of Evan's bathroom door wouldn't exactly make her look sexy.

Oh, maybe this is silly. They'd had sex. And it had been breathtaking. But that didn't mean the man wanted to be attacked as soon as he walked in the door after a hard day's work. She should just put back on her clothes and watch TV or something like a normal person until he got home. Then if he wanted to seduce her, he would.

So she stooped for her panties and bra, then rose back to her feet. And Evan's face appeared behind her in the mirror.

Oh God, she'd been caught! She swallowed heavily and her heart sank to her stomach.

How could she explain? She could tell him she was about to take a shower. Or she could fall back on the 'I like to lounge around in a robe' plan.

But no, no, no. Her eyes locked with Evan's in the mirror and a little voice whispered inside her. *The truth. Just tell him the truth. The truth is okay.*

And then it poured from her more effortlessly than she could have imagined. "I wanted to surprise you," she said, "so I took my clothes off. I thought it might excite you to come home and find me naked."

Evan's emerald eyes grew wild with passion as his briefcase drop to the floor with a *thud.* "Well," he breathed, "it worked."

Chapter Nine

———❧———

H E'D THOUGHT ABOUT her all day, waiting for this moment when he could see her again, touch her again—but he hadn't imagined...*this*. And he couldn't wait a second longer.

He ripped at his tie, finally yanking it off over his head, then he struggled with his shirt buttons. Cassandra watched him in the mirror, still and wide-eyed and naked and beautiful, until he said, "Help me do this."

She turned and worked at his belt and zipper as he continued with the damn shirt buttons whose number seemed to have doubled. When finally free of his clothes, he pushed her back against the sink, lifting her up on it. He pulled his hands away from her bare ass only to caress her breasts. When she leaned her head back and let out a deeply-pleasured sigh, it aroused him. God, he was crazy about this girl.

Gripping her hips, he pushed himself into her softness, making her cry out.

"Is it okay?" he asked, concerned.

She nodded and wrapped her legs around his waist,

squeezing him tighter against her and urging a groan from his throat.

"You feel so damn good," he breathed.

"So do you," she whispered back.

"Do you like having me inside you?" he asked, panting. He wanted to hear it.

He thrust into her and watched as she bit her lip, her eyes falling half shut and looked sultry as hell. "I like it a lot," she finally purred. She was meeting his thrusts now, pushing herself against him, beginning to set the rhythm of their sex.

"I want to make you come," he whispered.

She gasped, and opened her eyes wide, still moving on him. "Ohhh," she said. "Like when you were touching me last night. Except that now…mmm…"

"Now I'm deep inside you."

A few seconds later it happened. He watched as she closed her eyes and let her head drop back as jagged cries and whimpers filled the room with a staggering heat. The rocking of her body finally slowed until she grew still in his arms, and Evan tried to still his motions as well. Because he wanted this to last.

When she finally lifted her head and opened her eyes on him, a hot, playful little smile found her lips. She locked her arms around his neck tighter than before and raised to whisper in his ear. "I love you, Evan Hunt." Her breath tickled.

And he lost control, that fast. He began to thrust at her malleable body, his passion exploding inside her, his body pulsating with tremors of heat and light. "Oh baby, I love you too," he breathed, exhaustion gripping him. He leaned to rest his forehead on her shoulder.

After a moment of sweet recovery, he opened his eyes to find Cassandra watching him. He let his gaze slide from her face to her breasts, to their bodies still joined on the bathroom sink. He offered up a grin, suspecting it was tinged with wickedness. "I've never really liked surprises before—but suddenly I do."

They both laughed and she nuzzled his neck. And hell, it was just…nice. Nice and comfortable in a way he could get used to.

"Would you hate me if I wanted to stay in tonight?" he asked her then, eyebrows raised hopefully.

"No," she said. "After all, I can think of lots of ways for us to amuse ourselves." She lowered a warm kiss to his mouth as if he needed a reminder. "But what about dinner? I've worked up quite an appetite and I'm sorry to tell you that I'm not much of a chef."

"Not a problem," he said easily. "Gino's delivers."

She smiled.

"And if you're nice," he added, "I might even serve it to you in bed."

IT RAINED ALL weekend, but that didn't dampen Cassie's joy. She and Evan watched movies, fed each other popcorn, and snuggled beneath a blanket on the couch. She wore one of his sweatshirts when they shared an umbrella and a walk in the rain on the slick Chicago sidewalks. He made her breakfast in bed: an omelet in which he'd formed an adorable heart with tiny chunks of ham.

And Cassie spent the weekend learning how to love him back. "You have to remember," she told him on Saturday afternoon as they held hands in the rain, "this is all new for me, this being in love stuff."

Evan just laughed. "It's new for me, too. I've never fallen in love before either."

The admission left Cassie stunned and she couldn't resist smiling up at him. "So...I'm your first love?"

He nodded, lowering his eyes and looking uncharacteristically shy.

"But I'm not your first lover," she reminded him. "That's what I really meant. When I said love, I guess maybe I meant love *and* sex."

He turned thoughtful before saying, "I'm *glad* sex is new to you, honey. I mean—what guy wouldn't feel great to know that he was the only one?"

"Am I doing okay at it?" she asked him bluntly.

He smiled at her beneath the umbrella, then nodded slowly. "Making love to you would be amazing in any circumstance," he said, "but, um, yeah, you've loosened up quite a bit since the first time. And I like it."

They'd made love three more times since the bathroom liaison.

"Am I too aggressive?" she asked. She thought of the time he'd gone out for wine and take-out. Since her accidental surprise had worked so well, she'd decided this time to meet him at the door naked. And when he'd arrived, she'd ripped the bags from his arms and replaced them with herself.

He laughed at the question. "Um, no," he said, shaking his head. "Aggressive is good. I promise."

"Evan," Cassie said then, drawing her gaze from the wet sidewalk to peek up at him under the umbrella, "I was wondering something."

"What's that?" he asked easily, clearly not expecting a big question. But she had to ask him this.

"The first time we did it, you used protection. But since then..."

Shades of guilt passed through his eyes. "I know," he said, meeting her eyes before looking back ahead as they passed a woman walking a soggy poodle wearing a little yellow rain slicker. Once the woman and dog had passed, he explained. "But that time in the bathroom I was too worked up to even think about it. And since then, it's either been that or it seemed like there wasn't time. I'm usually not that way, I swear." He shook his head. "I'm usually the king of safe sex."

"Well," she reasoned, "at least you know you don't have to worry about catching any sexual diseases from *me*."

He shrugged. "Well, to put your mind at ease, the same is true for me. Because you're the first woman I've slipped up with. I promise."

"So then, I guess the only thing we might have to

worry about is…"

"Babies," he said shortly.

And Cassie shivered from the chill of the rain. "Evan, I don't know what I'd do if I got pregnant."

"It's not what *you* would do," he said. "It's what *we* would do. And what *we* would do is become a family. If that's what you wanted," he concluded.

Cassie didn't know what to say. She simply gripped his hand tighter and reached her other hand over to cling to his arm beneath the umbrella as his words echoed in her brain. *Become a family.* She wasn't particularly ready for motherhood, and still the thought sounded nice. At least maybe someday.

Then she swallowed nervously. How eager would Evan be to "become a family" with her if he knew the truth?

When they got too cold to walk anymore, they slipped into a deli and bought a fresh cheesecake to take home. They stood kissing in the rain while they waited for a bus to come and deliver them back to Evan's place. And even with the chill, Cassie didn't really want the moment to end. On the bus, she cuddled against him, liking the way his body heat overrode the moisture that had seeped into their skin.

When they got home, she peeled off her wet sweatshirt and Evan peeled off her wet bra. Then he took off his own shirt and they curled up on the couch beneath a cozy blanket and watched Casablanca.

After the movie and a short rainy-day nap, Evan rose

from the couch and returned with the cheesecake and a fork. They took turns taking bites and feeding each other, but soon a smudge of cheesecake found its way onto her breast where he licked it away. And soon neither one of them were thinking about cheesecake anymore.

They made love wrapped in a blanket on the couch where she straddled him until it happened again, until her body was shaken by those incredible waves of energy that made her abandon all other thought or feeling, those astounding sensations flooding her veins with a love for Evan so intense that it was almost painful. Painfully *good*. She collapsed on him after they had both finished.

She still hadn't gotten used to this—could a person *ever* get used to it? Now that she'd finally taken that step, crossed that line, she wanted to have sex with him all the time. She finally understood what all the fuss was about.

"Was it nice for you?" his sexy voice asked near her ear then. It was almost enough to make her want him already again, even though their bodies hadn't yet parted—he was still inside her.

She lifted her head from his shoulder and smiled playfully. "If I'd known it would feel this good," she teased, "I'd have started doing this a long time ago."

Though as soon as the playful words left her, she turned quickly serious. "No," she corrected herself. "I wouldn't have. I'd have waited. For someone special. For you. I'm so glad I waited."

WHEN CASSIE WOKE up the next morning, Evan's head lay on her chest. She looked down at him, sleeping peacefully, and raked her fingers through his hair. Who would have dreamed that a spilled glass of iced tea could lead to this perfect way of starting the day?

He stirred slightly, his eyes fluttering open. He lifted his gaze to hers with a lazy smile. "Good morning," he said groggily.

"Morning, sleepy head," she returned.

"Me?" he teased. "Looks like you're still in bed, too."

"Well, who wouldn't be, with a workout like the one you gave me last night?"

"Wait. I thought I was the one who'd been *given* the workout?"

"*You* started the thing with the cheesecake," she reminded him.

"Okay, maybe," he conceded. "But *you* started the one right after."

"Well then, who started the shower thing?"

"I believe that was also you," he replied smartly. "As I recall, you yanked me up from the couch and said you wanted to get wet together—which I thought was ironic, since we'd already spent half the day in the rain."

She bit her lip and pointed out teasingly, "Different kind of wet."

"Completely," he agreed.

"At any rate," she said, "I guess we both deserve a

little rest."

He gave a short nod. "Right. So I hope you understand that there will be no ham heart omelet today."

"No?" she asked, feigning disappointment with wide eyes. "But I loved that. It was so cute."

"Cute takes work, honey. And I just don't have the energy this morning."

She tilted her head sideways on the pillow. "I would settle for, say, cereal in bed. Or toast in bed."

He groaned. "I think I'd rather starve than get up." Then a heavy sigh left him. "Of course, it could be worse. It could be Monday."

Everybody hated Mondays, but Evan had sounded nearly depressed about the concept. "What's so awful about Monday?"

"Princess Cosmetics," he reminded her, sounding tired in a whole different way now.

"Wow," she said. "You act like it's the end of the world."

Evan's brow knit. And was she mistaken or…did he look almost a little startled somehow at her words? "What's wrong?" she asked.

"Nothing," he replied, running a hand back through his hair. "The stress is just getting to me, I guess. The, uh…low sales I told you about."

"I'm sure that can all be fixed, Evan," she told him.

"You make it sound easy." He looked more than a little skeptical.

"Well, *you* make it sound impossible," she argued.

Next to her, he propped up on one elbow, peering down at her. "I've been thinking, Cassandra, and I've figured out what the real problem is. The real problem is—what do I truly know about running a cosmetics company? I know lipstick and mascara as an outsider, but I have no personal experience with it. And I'm probably a lipstick and mascara *expert* compared to some of the old geezers on the board of directors.

"Still, I'm too immersed in the company—I have no objectivity. There's too damn much competition out there. And no fresh viewpoints inside. Half the people in the company have been there longer than I have and they've neglected to change with the times. Some of them aren't even qualified to be in their positions— they've simply moved up the ladder like kids who get passed onto higher grades without being able to read. I'm beginning to think the whole thing *is* impossible. And to be honest, some days I'd almost like to jump ship."

Evan's words left Cassie a little shocked. Would he really leave the company his mother founded and built into a household name? "Does that mean I've been thinking of more innovations in vain?" she asked.

Evan tilted his head, eyeing her suspiciously. "Wait a minute. When have you had time to think? I've been keeping you way too busy for your mind to be on something as trivial as cosmetics."

She gave him a flirtatious smile. "Don't worry. My mind is in the right place. But I've had a few minutes here and there—before sex, after sex. And I've come up with some more ideas. I mean, if you're interested—given that I don't really know the industry from a business perspective."

"Hell yes, I'm interested," he said. "Let's hear what you've got, honey—I'm all ears."

A few days ago, Cassie still would have felt nervous about sharing her views and suggestions, but the level of comfort she'd reached with Evan now made it easy, almost the same as if they were discussing anything else. "Okay, it's like this," she began. "If I'm not mistaken, Princess Cosmetics come in huge bottles and tubes, right?"

He shrugged, clearly thinking about that assessment. "They're sizable, yeah."

"I think that's impractical," Cassie informed him. "When I buy foundation, I don't want to be committed to it for life. Even the eye shadows seem much larger to me than other brands. Am I imagining that?"

"No," he said. "That's something we came up with a few years ago, when sales first started to dip. We wanted to give the consumer a lot for her money."

"Then decrease prices *and sizes*, Evan. I don't want to be locked in to wearing the same eye-shadow every day from now until eternity. I want the freedom of variety. In fact, even most standard size eye shadows are way too large to use in a reasonable period of time. Make them smaller so people can afford to buy more.

"And another thing. Eye shadow applicators. They wear out prematurely and then you have to go buy them separately just to keep using the same eye shadow. Why not include two or three in each package? Or replace them with small but better-quality shadow brushes. Women would love that."

He looked surprised to hear all this. "Yeah?"

"Absolutely," she assured him.

His eyes narrowed on her then. "You *have* been thinking about this, haven't you?" He sounded impressed, and inside her grew a glow of pride much like what she'd felt when she'd shared her ideas with him the other day.

"And there's more where that came from," she promised him, feeling confident now.

"Listen," he said with an introspective tilt of his head, "I've got an idea. I know you're busy looking for the perfect job and that you're on a heavy interviewing schedule. But would you consider doing me a favor and coming into work with me a couple of days this week? I'd really like to get some of your ideas in writing. You could work with Miriam on a presentation and take your suggestions to the board."

Cassie swallowed. Blinked. Almost couldn't breathe. "You want me to make a *presentation*? To the *board*?"

"Absolutely," he said with a succinct nod. "You've got some really interesting ideas and you present them clearly and persuasively. Much more so than I could. Let's face it. How the hell would *I* know these things? And more importantly, how the hell could I convince the board that this is what women want?"

She appreciated his confidence in her, but calling in an outsider with no experience seemed like a drastic move for a CEO to take just because sales had decreased a little. "But Evan—"

"Look at you, Cassandra. You're a beautiful woman with good taste and a great education to back you up. Harvard Business," he said, more to himself than to her. "That'll knock 'em dead."

Cassie winced. "Yeah," she said, her voice grown mousy. "Harvard. Knock 'em dead." *And while you're at it, put me out of my misery, too.* She sighed heavily.

"Oh," he said, hearing the hesitation in her voice. "Look, if you don't want me to mention Harvard, that's fine. I understand if you want to stand on your own merit."

Ha. Stand on my own merit. What *merit?* But it was a quick fix so she'd take it. She'd gotten frightening good at spotting those and grabbing onto them lately. Prompting her to say, "Yeah—I think it might be better that way."

"So you'll do it?" he asked with a gorgeous smile that nearly melted her.

But melting smile or not, she still had doubts. Serious ones. "Evan," she began, "won't they wonder why you've called in a..." What *was* she exactly? The word 'fraud' came to mind.

"A consultant?" Evan said. "Cassandra, I'm sure you know companies use consultants all the time."

"But I'm *not* one."

"Sure you are. I've been consulting with you, haven't I?"

Evan watched Cassandra tilt her head and peer up into his eyes from the pillow where she still lay. He took a deep breath, sensing her growing concern. She obviously knew there was something he wasn't telling her.

"I know this must seem like a desperate move," he said quietly.

And she replied, "Exactly."

And he knew this would be a good time to tell her the real truth about his company's woes. Who cared if she wasn't on the board of directors? She seemed more invested in the company's success than most of those stodgy old men, anyway. He sighed, trying to summon the words. "Things at Princess are...well, not terrific right now."

"I know," she said. "You've told me."

But not everything. Not even close.

Maybe it would be easier to simply blurt it out. *Princess is about to go under.*

But he just couldn't do it.

And he wasn't even sure why.

After all, wouldn't it be a relief of sorts to get it off his chest? To share it with the woman he was in a great—albeit new—relationship with? Wasn't that kind of sharing what you were supposed to do in a relationship?

"Well," he began, trying, "maybe they're...even less terrific than you think."

"Oh," she said, sounding a little sad to hear that. "Well, just how unterrific are they?"

"Um…pretty damn unterrific," he said, faltering, and wishing he could hide the worry that surely dripped from his eyes.

In fact, now he almost wished he hadn't even started the conversation. After all, would Cassandra still want him if he was suddenly a failure?

Oh, *that* was why he couldn't just spit it out. Hell— talk about figuring something out. He was used to feeling successful in life, used to wearing that persona. He'd never really known any other. So maybe he didn't want the woman he'd fallen for so hard to think of him as a loser.

"Unterrific *this quarter*," he then heard himself explain. "Things are bad this quarter and the board is on my back about it, worried about our annual figures. That's all."

"I'm sure everyone has bad quarters now and then," she suggested easily. And despite himself, he was glad he hadn't spilled the beans about how bad things were. He didn't even like having to face it himself, after all—why would he want someone who thought highly of the corporation to have to face it, too?

"Yeah," he said, leaving it at that.

"And I'm sure things will get better." She punctuated that thought with a lovely smile, all the hope in the world glittering in her eyes.

"With your help, maybe," he said then, coming back

to his proposition. "Will you do this for me? Will you present your ideas to my board and knock their socks off with ways to get Princess back up on top of the cosmetics throne again?"

Cassie drew in a deep breath. What on earth could she say?

Evan's eyes swam with anxiety. And she had to admit it was the opportunity of a lifetime. The idea pretty much terrified her, of course, but Jewel had been right that night at the banquet—she had to learn to move among these people if she wanted to be one of them.

So she mustered every ounce of courage inside her and said, "Sure, Evan. I'll do it."

After which she instantly realized the powerful position in which she'd just place herself. He owed her now. "On one condition," she added.

And he read her mind and began to drag himself out of bed. "All right," he said grudgingly. "One ham heart omelet, coming up."

BY MONDAY MORNING, it was even harder to crawl out of Evan's bed and leave him than it had been on Friday. But at least she'd covered all the bases in advance this time. Sunday night she'd told him that she had a dance class at the gym again on Monday. He'd groaned about it, but respected her pretended efforts to keep in shape and care about her body. She'd told him she would go to work with him on Tuesday and Wednesday, thereby giving her a chance to get advice from Jewel and lie to Eddie beforehand.

"He *what?*" Jewel exploded with excitement in the break room.

"Shhh," Cassie said. "Keep it down. Eddie can't hear this. Anyway, yes—Evan asked me to come to his office and present my ideas to his board of directors."

Jewel beamed with joy. "That's great, kid! Really! I'm so proud of you."

Still, Cassie winced. "Proud of me for lying my way into Evan's bed or proud of me for lying my way into Evan's company?"

Jewel planted her hands on her hips. "Lying didn't get you into either of those places and you know it. Lying was just a mistake you made in the beginning that you haven't found a way to fix yet. Him being crazy about you is what got you into his bed. And brains," she said, tapping her temple, "is what's getting you into that big pink building."

"Maybe," Cassie sighed. "But this is getting so complicated. And now I've got even *more* problems."

"What problems are those? I'm sure we can fix them."

Thank God for Jewel! Her can-do attitude always helped Cassie get through tricky situations—more lately, of course, than ever before.

"First," she said, keeping her voice down, "I'm going to have to lie to Eddie about where I am."

"A white lie at most," Jewel justified it, waving a

nonchalant hand down through the air. "And I'm sure you're not the first person to put one over on the Ed-meister. Besides, I forgot to tell you, he hired a new girl for the weekends, and we're training her today. I'll ask her to come in tomorrow and Wednesday, too."

"All right, one problem down," Cassie said, letting out a tentative sigh of relief. "But I also need two business suits and I don't have the money to buy them."

Jewel thought for a moment and they both spoke at the same time. "Irma!"

"I'll get her on the phone right now," Jewel said.

"Jewel, it's six AM," Cassie pointed out. "Most reasonable human beings are not awake yet."

"Don't worry," Jewel said, ignoring the protest and dialing. "Irma and I are like *this*." She crossed her fingers.

And a few minutes later Jewel informed Cassie that they had an appointment with Irma at Marshall Fields today at five o'clock. "Is that too late for you to go home to your lover man?"

"No," Cassie said, shaking her head. "And I won't even have to lie. I'll just tell him I was at Marshall Fields getting a new suit for tomorrow."

"Perfect," Jewel said.

"Now to deal with Eddie," Cassie groaned, looking toward the kitchen where he was just starting to prepare for the day. "Wish me luck."

Jewel cocked her head sideways and grinned. "If you ask me, Cass, you already got more of that than most of us. Just keep on keepin' the faith."

Cassie headed into the kitchen to find her boss lining up cartons of eggs and plates of sausage links and bacon for the breakfast orders to come. "Eddie, I need to talk to you for a minute," she said.

Eddie lifted his head. "What can I do for you, Cass?"

"Well, the thing is...I've, um, had a death in the family."

Now he stopped what he was doing and raised his eyes. "I'm sorry to hear that." He sounded more concerned and sincere than she'd expected. Which made her feel guiltier than she'd expected.

But she pressed on, having no other choice. "It was my old Aunt Thelma," she lied. "Back in Hargrove."

"Were you close to her?"

Oh geez, questions. She hadn't expected questions. "Yes," she said, "I was."

And to her further surprise, Eddie went so far as to lift a hand to her shoulder as he said, "I'm real sorry for your loss, Cassie."

Oh crap. She felt like dirt.

"I remember when my Aunt Betsy died," Eddie went on. "She looked out for me a lot when I was a kid and it was tough losing her."

Oh God, Cassie thought. Now her lie had made Eddie confide in her. Bond with her.

"Thought my mother would never quit crying," he added. "It was a rough time for the whole family. She was the lynch pin, ya know? The one who really held the family together. It was cancer."

I am lower than dirt. I am pond scum. She couldn't stand to hear any more. "Well, the thing is, Eddie, I need a couple days off to go to Kentucky for the funeral."

"Not another word, Cassie," he said, holding up one hand. "You take all the time you need."

Cassie was dumbfounded. And horrified—at herself. "Thanks, Eddie," she mumbled. Then she excused herself from the kitchen, trying not to dwell on what a pond-scummy dirtball she had become.

THE REST OF the morning passed without mishap. Cassie and Jewel took turns training the new waitress, Trudy, a short redhead with an affinity for bubble gum. Jewel asked Trudy if she'd mind working in Cassie's place on Tuesday and Wednesday and she agreed. Now all Cassie had to do was get those suits from Irma this afternoon and she'd be set for her two days in the corporate world at Princess Cosmetics. Thoughts of actually having something to put on a resume danced in her head.

When the noon hour rolled around, the diner became swamped. A bus of senior citizens on a city tour pulled up at twelve o'clock sharp and the old folks filed in, completely filling Jewel's section. Cassie wished she could help her friend out, but she had her hands full with the other half of the restaurant, not to mention prodding Trudy to take some initiative—and some food orders, on her own.

"Order up, Cass," Eddie said through the window as

she returned with four more tickets.

"Can you deliver that to table seven while I fill some drink orders?" Cassie asked Trudy. Trudy didn't move quickly, but she *did* deliver the food.

Half an hour later, the rush on Cassie's side of the diner had begun to diminish. All the customers had their food and a few of the booths were even empty. Unfortunately for Jewel, the slow moving senior citizens were just getting started. "That grandma in the crocheted sweater has changed her order three times now," Jewel muttered beneath her breath as she moved past Cassie.

Cassie was about to help Jewel pour coffee for the old folks when the front door opened. And four suits walked in. And one of them was Evan.

Chapter Ten

———∞———

I T WAS SO unexpected, and so horrible, that for a moment Cassie hoped she might simply be imagining things. But she wasn't imagining anything. Evan was really here. Her chest tightened in terror and her heart began to race as she ducked through the doorway that led to the kitchen.

This couldn't be happening! It simply couldn't! She peeked around the corner and watched as Evan and his three associates sat down in the same booth as last week, the same booth where her fateful first meeting with him had taken place. *My God—was it really only been last week?*

But there was no time to reflect on how quickly her life had turned upside down. She had to figure out what to do.

And then the solution hit her. Trudy! Who was just coming out of the bathroom, so as she moved past, Cassie grabbed her sleeve. "Trudy," she said, still careful to stay out of view, "I need a favor."

Trudy blew a bubble, then popped it with her index

finger. "What?"

"See those guys over there? The handsome ones in the suits?"

Trudy tossed a glance toward Evan's table, then nodded.

"Can you take their order for me? It would be a big help."

"No offense," Trudy said around her gum, "but you don't look real busy, and I don't feel real comfortable taking orders yet. I'd rather just watch you."

"Come on," Cassie said. "Just do this for me. You gotta get your feet wet at some point today, and there's no better time than the present."

"I don't think so," Trudy replied.

For heaven's sake, why had Eddie even hired this belligerent girl? "Come on," Cassie said again, trying not to beg. "It's a big tip, I promise."

"Nope," Trudy said. Then she blew another bubble. Cassie reached out her finger and popped it in frustration—then ducked down and snuck out of the kitchen and behind the counter in the dining room.

Stooping down and pretending to fiddle with napkins and coffee stirrers stored there, she tried desperately to think of a plan. She'd come this far—she couldn't blow it now. And when Evan found out the truth, it certainly couldn't be like this. She had to find the right way to explain, the right time to break it to him.

Then her eyes landed on something beneath the counter—the lost and found bin. And it gave her an idea. A hideously stupid idea. But it was better than no idea at all, so she studied the bin's contents and ran with it. *There isn't much to work with, but I can do this.*

Locating a navy blue ski cap, she pulled it down over her head, shoving her blond ponytail up inside. Then she found a pair of sunglasses.

Even so—Evan knew her way too well; sunglasses would never hide enough of her face. And the only real face-covering item she dredged up was a ridiculous-looking cat mask made mostly of bright pink feathers and glitter. It would have to do. She slipped the elastic string over her head to hold it on. It covered her face from forehead to nose.

That left her mouth. And like the rest of her, Evan knew that part of her—maybe better than some others. He'd been kissing it all weekend, after all. And sometimes he traced it with his fingertips when they were lying in bed together after sex. Therefore it had to be hidden.

In pure desperation mode, she reached for her purse on the bottom shelf behind the counter and dug until she found a tube of fuchsia lipstick. She smeared on lips way too large. She didn't have the luxury of a mirror, but thought it was probably better that way—if she could see herself, she'd never have the guts to go through with this.

As a finishing touch, she grabbed a pair of bright yellow rubber gloves that she and Jewel used for heavy cleaning jobs. Just in case Evan might recognize her hands.

Cassie took a deep breath and rose up from behind the counter. The first person she saw was Jewel, who blinked at her, probably to make sure she wasn't seeing things. "What the hell are you doing?" She'd never seen her friend look more taken aback.

"It's Evan," Cassie said. "He's here. And Trudy won't wait on him."

Jewel scowled at the new girl and looked like she was about to say something nasty—when a member of the senior group tapped a spoon on a water glass. "Waitress! Waitress!"

"I'm sorry, kid," Jewel said. "I'd gladly help you out, but I got the blue hair convention going over here, claiming their soup is cold and their water is warm and basically making me feel responsible for everything that's ever gone wrong in their lives."

"I understand," Cassie said. And she knew she'd better get a move on it, too, before Eddie yelled out her name. She swallowed nervously, reached into her apron for her order pad, and strolled boldly up to Evan's table.

She was greeted with stares of shock that slowly turned to cautious amusement.

"Can I take your order?" she asked from behind her feathers, deepening her voice dramatically and letting the downhome Kentucky accent from the community where she'd grown up blast through.

The man to Evan's right spoke first, wearing a slight grin. "What's the mask for?"

"I'm getting ready for Mardi Gras," she claimed.

"Mardi Gras isn't for months yet," he said.

Cassie swallowed, then resumed her deep tone. "Well, I'm a real party girl. Couldn't wait for the fun to begin. Woohoo!" she added for good measure.

"Interesting hat," another of Evan's friend's observed with a smirk of amusement.

"I'm going as…a cat burglar," Cassie came up with, drawing a few chuckles from the men.

"What are the gloves for?" the first man asked. Wow, he was just Mr. Twenty Questions, wasn't he?

And then it hit her—a much better lie than the ones she'd just been telling. She kept her accent and deep voice in place to say, "Actually, the truth is, my ex is here right now, eating lunch. Real stalker type, if ya know what I mean. He doesn't know I work here and I want to keep it that way, ya know?"

This made all four men go quiet and look more serious, until the first one said, "Oh wow, I see. Not sure this is the best way not to draw attention to yourself, but…"

"But it was all I had," she said. "And I'm pretty sure it's working."

"More power to you then," the guy replied, and finally, to her relief, gave his order.

When it was Evan's turn to speak, he looked up at her—and then slowly tilted his head to the side.

She took a deep breath and waited, saying a silent prayer. She *thought* it was working anyway. But as he narrowed those wonderful green eyes on her, her heart pounded so hard she feared it would leap from her chest.

Could it be? Could Evan be recognizing her eyes? Her chin? Her stupidly disguised voice? She felt herself begin to tremble and worked very hard to hold still.

"I'll have the roast beef plate," he said at last. And Cassie let out her breath in one heavy *whoosh*.

Yet along with relief came...a crushing heartbreak. Somehow, hearing his voice, there, like that, while in disguise—not his lover but simply some goofy waitress—killed something inside her. Because in truth that's all she actually was: some goofy waitress who he really knew nothing about.

"Iced tea to drink," he added then.

Iced tea! Cassie's heart plummeted in a mixture of love and deceit.

She somehow maintained her composure through the other men's orders, inspired only by the fact that nothing would be worse than a woman wearing big lips and a cat mask breaking down in tears.

When she finally returned to the counter, Cassie had reached her breaking point. She shoved the orders into Trudy's hand and snapped, "When these come up, deliver them. Got it?"

Trudy was shocked into submission, probably from Cassie's appearance as much as her snappish tone. "Okay."

She rushed to the bathroom in the back, ripping off her disguise as she went. Once there, she clawed at the toilet paper until she got enough to wipe the ridiculous lipstick off her mouth. Then came the tears, falling down her cheeks and dripping onto her pink uniform to create blotches of a deeper shade. She couldn't think straight anymore, couldn't reason—she could only feel. She sank to her knees without knowing and knelt on the bathroom floor, her face in her hands.

She looked up when the door opened. Jewel stood over her, her eyes fraught with concern. "Cass, are you okay?"

Cassie tried to sniff back her tears. "I'll be fine."

"I heard you sobbing all the way in the dining room."

Oh Lord! "You did?" Cassie hadn't realized she was making any noise at all.

Jewel stooped down until she was eye level with Cassie. "Did Evan know it was you?" she whispered.

And Cassie shook her head. "No, I'm just...sick...about everything—all the lies."

"I know," Jewel said softly, reaching out to squeeze her hand.

"I really love him, Jewel," Cassie said through her tears, then tried to sniff them back. "I mean, this isn't just about chasing around some rich guy—I'm completely and totally in love with him. And I'm so *tired*. I'm tired of the charade and I'm angry at myself for living like this. When he finds out, he'll absolutely hate me. And I still don't know how I can ever tell him."

Jewel reached out to hug Cassie, who started crying again on her friend's shoulder. "That's all right, kid,"

Jewel said. "Just let it all out."

Yet Cassie sniffed again, lifting her head and reaching for toilet paper to blow her nose. "Thanks, but I'd better get back out there," she said. She swiped more toilet paper across her eyes to dry them. "Eddie's probably livid by now."

Jewel shook her head. "No. He feels bad for you. He thinks you're upset about your dead aunt."

And Cassie burst back into tears.

"Listen," Jewel said, "I gotta get back out there to the wrinkle crew, but you take a few minutes for yourself. Stay in here for a little while. Give Evan a chance to eat his lunch and leave. Eddie'll understand."

Jewel shut the door behind her, leaving Cassie in the bathroom by herself. She supposed at this point it was a good idea to wait, like Jewel had said. Besides, it would give her a chance to compose herself.

She turned to look at herself in the mirror. What a mess. Her face was red and her eye makeup was every-where except where it was supposed to be. Her hair was strewn in every direction, much of it having come out of her ponytail holder. She turned the faucet on and splashed cool water on her face. Then she made a new, neater ponytail.

And she thought of the day she'd met Evan. She'd been in the break room playing with her hair, wishing it were more elegant and that she were more classy so that she might fit in with men like him. Funny—as it turned out, it didn't take floofy hair or expensive clothes or a large vocabulary to fit in with Evan. He loved her for the person she was. Well, for the person he *thought* she was. If only she hadn't started spinning that stupid web of lies trying to impress him.

CASSIE WATCHED MAC scarf down a fish sandwich as he leaned against the dirty metal Dumpster behind Fast Eddie's.

"Don't eat so fast," she told him. "You'll choke yourself."

"Hungry," he confided between bites.

She sighed, disturbed to know that meant Mac had had a long, hard weekend, all while she'd been having the most wonderful time of her life.

And then, out of the blue, it hit her. Oh no! She hadn't gone to the shelter this weekend! Not on Saturday. Not on Sunday. She gasped at the realization. She couldn't believe it had entirely slipped her mind. She hadn't even called anyone to let them know they'd be shorthanded!

Mac looked up from his fish. "What?"

She couldn't fathom her own carelessness, her selfishness. "Mac, I'm so sorry."

"What are you sorry for?" He looked confused.

"The shelter. I wasn't there." She tried to swallow back her guilt. "I told you I'd check on that guy for you and then I didn't show. Mac, I apologize. Can you ever forgive me?"

Mac's eyes met hers. "You don't gotta be sorry, Cassie. You don't owe me nothin'."

"Well, sure I do," she told him. "We're friends, aren't we? And friends should be able to depend on each other to keep promises, to do what they say they're going to."

Mac shook his head, ever-understanding. "Aw, don't be so hard on yourself. Nobody can be perfect all the time."

Cassie took his words as a compliment she didn't deserve as she peered sheepishly up at him from beneath lowered eyelids. "I don't think I'm perfect *any* of the time, Mac. In fact, lately I'm far from it. And it all leads back to my lies. I've been so busy maintaining my double life that I've been neglecting things, and people, who are important to me."

"Still haven't told that fella the truth yet, huh?"

She suddenly found it hard to meet his gaze, so she cast her glance downward, shaking her head.

"You care about him?" he asked her.

"Yes," she said. "In fact, I even…well, I've fallen completely in love with him."

"Then you gotta tell him the truth, Cassie," he told her, shaking his head. "I know I went easy on you about it before, but I see this thing's gotten serious now. You gotta come clean before it eats you alive."

"It's *already* eating me alive," she told him. "And I *want* to tell him the truth. Truly, I do. But how? How do you tell someone you've completely misled them?"

"Guess you gotta figure that out on your own," he

somberly replied.

She sighed, kicking at a pebble with the toe of her gym shoe, then decided to move on to a topic she might be able to handle more effectively. "Were things okay at the shelter this weekend? Is that guy still bothering you?"

Mac shook his head. "Nope. Now he's bothering Sally and her girl."

Cassie's stomach twisted. Sally was a shy young mother about her own age. Her absence had ultimately let down not only Mac, but Sally, too. "That's it," she replied. "I have an appointment after work today, but after that I'm stopping by the shelter and talking to somebody about this guy. And I'll check on Sally while I'm there."

Mac nodded. "Thanks, Cassie. That's good of you."

"Can you ever forgive me for letting you down, Mac?" she tilted her head to ask.

In response, he lifted his gaze, wearing a suddenly mischievous smile. "Piece of chocolate pie might make it up to me."

And Cassie couldn't help releasing a small laugh. "All right," she conceded. "This once. But don't expect me to make a habit of this." Then she turned toward the back door of the diner, ready to go get Mac a piece of pie.

EVAN LAY RELAXING on the couch in a T-shirt and workout pants, waiting for Cassandra to come home. He wondered how she spent her days. She seemed to be busy with her gym and her extensive job search, but the hours she appeared to devote to the two activities were extensive.

He supposed he should admire her tenacity. And really, he did. But he'd been disappointed to come from work early to spend time with her only to find the condo empty. He'd even run by *her* place, thinking perhaps she's stopped there to pick up some business clothes, but he'd gotten no answer at the big steel door.

Rising from the couch, he headed toward his pantry. He wasn't a great cook, but decent—so perhaps they could share a nice dinner at home, then a relaxing evening together before her first big day at the office tomorrow.

He truly respected her ideas for Princess, but more than that, there was something in the way she delivered them—a sense of authority that made him instantly believe she was right. It was a quality his mother had possessed, too. And it was that—along with the ideas— that he felt might win the board over and allow him to start implementing big, much-needed changes.

She had no idea how much he appreciated her willingness to try to bail him out of a jam that he should have taken steps to prevent years ago. Not that she knew how big the jam was. Or the weight he placed on her presentation. He couldn't believe he'd been that close to the truth and not managed to tell her.

He sighed. His untruthfulness aside, he hoped the board would be as impressed by her ideas as he had been.

They could be a damn inflexible bunch of old men.

Evan found half a box of spaghetti and a jar of marinara sauce, then dug in the freezer until he came up with some garlic rolls, as well as some ground beef he could thaw in the microwave, then season and roll into meatballs. Luckily, he had some red wine on hand which he thought would make the simple meal seem a little more romantic. He wanted to show Cassandra his appreciation, even if he couldn't quite explain to her why this felt so important—and hell, he wanted her to know how much he valued having her in his life period.

He smiled, thinking of Miriam's reaction to the new him. This afternoon, she'd told him she couldn't get over how relaxed he'd been these past few work days, and how much more he smiled, despite all the trouble at work. "Love is good for you," she'd told him with a knowing wink. He had to agree.

As he poured the sauce into a pot, his stomach growled. He'd eaten quickly today, hurrying back to an afternoon meeting, and he'd ended up leaving half his lunch behind.

The thought spurred his memory of that crazy waitress today in the feathered mask. How bizarre.

And that brought to mind the cute, nervous little waitress who had spilled iced tea on him in the same diner last week. That seemed like ages ago now. He wondered if she'd made it through her first week on the job. Maybe not.

Evan had just started to form the meatballs when the

phone rang. He wiped his hands on a dish towel and answered. "Hello?"

"Evan, it's Cassandra."

Just hearing her voice made him smile. "Hi, honey. Where are you?"

"I'm gonna be a little late. I'm getting something new to wear tomorrow."

He chuckled lightly. "You don't have to do that. Whatever you've been wearing on interviews will be fine."

"Well," she began, "I've been needing some new suits anyway and...I just want to look nice and make a good impression."

"All right," he said, thinking her adorable. "But hurry home. I miss you."

CASSIE WONDERED HOW she'd caught herself in time when Evan had answered the phone. She'd nearly said, *Evan, it's Cassie.* Right as the name had started to leave her mouth, she'd somehow remembered to spit out the elongated version.

After the call, she and Jewel rushed to Marshall Fields where Irma led them through the entire women's suit department. "Professional but fresh," she told Irma of the look she was seeking. "Sophisticated, but not unapproachable."

She was soon outfitted in a vibrant red suit with a stylish shape and stunning neckline. She decided it would be perfect for starting her business career tomorrow. "It looks eager but educated," she said to the other two women.

Next, she chose a simple but elegant form-fitting black suit with a hemline that showed off her legs a bit. This, Cassie proclaimed to Jewel and Irma, would be her presentation suit for Wednesday. It looked serious and smart, but also feminine.

To go with them, Irma loaned her a pair of simple but stylish black heels, a black purse with a dainty shoulder strap, and coordinating jewelry. Cassie was in love with her selections, sorry that they would all have to be returned.

"Don't go advertising this," Irma warned her as she drew long plastic covers over the suits. "It's a lot easier to justify loaning things out for a big society event than for a day at the office, so this stuff is going out of here off the books."

"You don't know how much I appreciate it, Irma," Cassie told her, taking her hand.

"You're saving her butt big time," Jewel added.

After leaving Marshall Fields, Cassie lugged her borrowed suits and accessories down to the Sunshine House.

"Cassie, we missed you this weekend," said Ann, the shelter's director, when Cassie walked in the door.

She knew she must look forlorn. "I'm really sorry, Ann. I was…unexpectedly detained," she explained lamely.

"That's all right—don't worry about it." Ann smiled.

"You're usually one of our most dependable volunteers."

Cassie returned the smile, appreciating that Ann put her at ease, and then got down to business. "Listen, Ann, I stopped by to check on Sally. Mac tells me someone has been bothering him, and now her. Do you know anything about it?"

Ann nodded. "I spoke with Sally about it earlier today. I've talked to the young man in question and have agreed to give him one more chance, but if I get anymore complaints, he's out."

Cassie knew they had to be reasonable, but she hated risking the other residents' safety. "Could you try to keep a close eye on him?" Cassie asked. "As a special favor to me? I sort of promised Mac I'd take care of it."

Ann's expression was comforting. "Don't worry, Cassie. I'll handle it." Then her eyes narrowed with concern. "But I've warned you about getting attached to the residents. It's not a healthy practice."

Cassie sighed. "I know, but what can I say? Mac's my buddy."

"I understand," Ann said with a nod. "After all, if we didn't care, we wouldn't be here, right?"

Somewhat appeased about the situation, Cassie finally caught a bus for Evan's place. And as she was about to walk into the building's lobby, she realized—oh crap—that she still wore her pink uniform. She stomped her foot on the city sidewalk in frustration. Ugh!

So then she trudged two blocks up the street to the nearest convenient store, borrowed the key to a rather gritty bathroom, and changed into the jeans she'd been toting around all day just for that purpose. And she supposed she should just be thankful she'd noticed her mistake when she still had time to fix it.

Exhaustion gripped her by the time she finally walked down the quiet hall from the elevator to Evan's condo. Her arms ached from lugging all her things. And her feet felt like they'd worn away to mere nubs at the bottoms of her legs. She hadn't even the strength to dig out her key, so she rang the bell and listened to it chime on the other side of the door.

The sight of Evan's welcoming smile was almost enough to revive her. But not quite. "Help me," she said, motioning to the bags and hangers weighing her down.

He quickly relieved her of some of the things she carried. "Looks like you've been a busy girl."

She nodded, then smiled when she thought of the suits. "I hope you like the stuff I picked out."

"I'm sure I'll love it," he said. Then he looked down at the brown bag he held in his arm. "What's in here?" he asked, starting to reach inside.

Cassie let the things she still held fall to the floor, then yanked the bag from his arm. "Nothing," she said. "Just dirty...gym clothes." The bag actually held her dirty pink uniform. She couldn't believe she'd let Evan get so close to it.

"I need to do some laundry later," he said. "Want me to toss yours in, too?"

"No!" she said, too emphatically.

His eyes went wide—and then he laughed, misunderstanding her alarm. "Don't worry," he said. "I'm good with laundry. I don't mix brights and whites, and I know when to use the gentle cycle."

Cassie took a deep breath and tried to smile. *Calm down. Get this back under control. Like you always do.* "Thanks, Evan," she said gently. "Really. But...I'm pickier than you can even imagine. I wash everything by hand."

"That's pretty picky," he agreed.

Thank God. He wasn't going to keep insisting.

"And...sorry if I snapped at you," she said. "I'm just tired, I guess."

Evan's gaze softened on her. "You've had a long day, haven't you, honey?" She nodded and he reached out to squeeze her shoulder.

"I just want to relax," she told him, rolling down the top of the paper bag to shield its contents, then lowering it to the floor behind her with the other stuff she'd carried in.

"In a little while we'll snuggle up on the couch and take it easy," he told her. "But in the meantime, I've kept dinner warm."

Cassie quickly forgot her near-disaster, letting her eyes widen in a combination of gratefulness and guilt. "You made dinner?"

He nodded, guiding her to the table. "Nothing special. Just spaghetti and meatballs."

"I *love* spaghetti and meatballs," she told him, looking up into those still-piercing green eyes. "And I love *you*, too."

As Evan slid his arms warmly around her, she pressed her body lightly into his. "Do you know you're perfect?" she asked, reaching up to run her fingers through his hair.

"I know I want you," he said throatily near her ear. "Right here, right now, on the dining room table."

Cassie's blood thickened at the suggestion, but another part of her knew that such an indulgence would best be saved for another time.

"Evan," she began, "would you absolutely hate me if I told you I was completely exhausted?" She mooned up at him with puppy dog eyes.

And he groaned in frustration, but smiled down at her anyway. "I'd already forgotten. See what you do to me? But I suppose I can forgive you," he added sweetly. "And I guess we'd better eat this stuff before it gets cold."

Cassie couldn't believe Evan had whipped them up such a nice little dinner, even lighting candles and serving wine in stemmed glasses. And she really *did* want to make love to him. On the dining room table or anywhere else he wanted. But her body simply wasn't up for it tonight. And all this running around was simply one more consequence of her stupid lies.

She enjoyed the dinner Evan had prepared and thanked him for his thoughtfulness. But by the time they moved into the living room to watch a little TV, wine and general weariness combined with her worries about tomorrow to make Cassie fall asleep nearly as soon as she settled into Evan's arms.

And when he woke her later for just long enough to change into one of his old T-shirts and climb into bed, she couldn't deny that this whole charade was beginning to take a toll on her, body and soul.

But I can't let that wear me down now—because tomorrow is my big chance, and the next two days might be some of the most important of my life!

Chapter Eleven

———∞———

CASSIE TRIED NOT to be a basket case the next morning. After all, a graduate of the Harvard Business School should not be bouncing off the walls over the prospect of spending a couple of days in an office environment.

She stood before the mirror in Evan's bedroom studying herself. Her red suit fit like a charm, and her makeup, applied from Princess samples Evan had brought home for her to use in preparation for her presentation, made her eyes pop and her lips shine. She'd pulled her hair back from her face in a loose chignon and felt professional but pretty.

She met Evan's gaze in the mirror as he exited the bathroom, a towel wrapped around his waist. He looked hard and wet and good enough to eat. But she couldn't think about that now.

"You look terrific," he told her.

"Honest?" she asked.

He laughed in his typical easy way. "I've probably never mentioned how much professional women turn me on, have I?"

I knew it, I just knew it. "No," she told him flirtatiously, "but I guess that's convenient." *Sort of. If I wasn't such a fake.*

"And if I dropped my towel," he said, flirting back, "you could see the proof."

His words set Cassie's blood racing. She definitely wanted to see the proof. But instead, she just took a deep breath, then blew it back out. "Evan," she begged, "please don't say things like that right now. I'm nervous and I can't afford to be distracted."

"You never know," he said, moving up behind her to massage her shoulders lightly, "a little distraction might do you some good. Although I don't know why you're so nervous."

"It's just my nature," she claimed, not quite meeting his eyes in the mirror this time.

He flashed and encouraging smile. "I have no doubt you'll do great, honey. I have complete faith in you."

Ugh. Evan surely would have been stunned to know her stomach wrenched painfully at his sweet words. *He had faith in her! Faith!* She sighed and wished she were a better person.

After leaning in to kiss her on the cheek, he started dressing for work—and she remained at the mirror, still studying her reflection. In one sense she was frightened, and in another she felt like a complete impostor, a total sham. But in a way that slowly transcended all those bad feelings, the longer she looked at herself, the stronger she began to feel. She belonged in that suit—it felt right. And she belonged in an office, making decisions, making things work—even though she hadn't done it yet, that felt right, too. "I can do this," she whispered to herself. "I can do it."

Cassie took one last glance at her suit. It was a heck of a lot nicer than the stupid pink uniform she wore to sling hash at Fast Eddie's and just wearing such nice apparel was enough to help build her confidence.

And then suddenly she remembered the paper bag that contained her waitress uniform. She'd never picked it up last night after setting it on the kitchen floor, having left it with her purse and another bag containing *actual* workout clothes!

As casually as she could manage, she turned to exit the bedroom—and once she'd left Evan's view, she dashed to the kitchen. She turned the corner, ready to snatch the bag up and find a good hiding place for it—but it was gone!

Cassie's breath grew instantly labored as her eyes darted around the kitchen in search of the incriminating sack. But it was nowhere in sight.

"Um, Evan?" she yelled, trying to sound perfectly happy—as opposed to panicky.

"Yeah?" he yelled back from the bedroom.

"Have you, uh, seen the bag with my dirty clothes in it?"

"Yeah, honey. I picked it up last night."

Her panic rose, but she kept attempting to sound

calm. "You picked it up?"

"Yeah. I stuck it in the bathroom."

In the bathroom? Evan had just come out of the bathroom. Which must mean…he hadn't looked inside! And he was acting perfect normal, so of course he hadn't seen anything that had struck him as odd.

Cassie breathed a huge sigh of relief, and promised herself she'd be more careful from now on. Then she headed back to the bedroom and walked past Evan into the bathroom, just to make sure. The bag set next to the hamper. It remained rolled down.

Still, this had been way too close for comfort. And Cassie didn't need any reminders, today of all days, about what a liar she had become.

"Don't look so worried," Evan said cheerfully, approaching behind her.

"What?" she asked, looking up into his gorgeous, green eyes.

"I won't touch your delicates, I promise," he told her playfully. Then he moved in for a warm, morning kiss that sent ribbons of desire curling through her body as usual. His hands dropped from her waist to her behind just before he pulled back to offer a sexy-as-sin grin. "At least not the ones in the bag."

AN HOUR LATER Evan and Cassie strolled briskly up the sidewalk approaching the Princess building amidst a flurry of activity. Women and men in suits moved in every direction on the city street, but many joined them, heading toward the revolving doors that led to Princess Cosmetics. Evan carried a briefcase and Cassie's hand's felt empty—she wanted to latch onto his arm, but she knew it wasn't professional behavior to cling to the boss, so she fought back the urge and tried to look confident as she walked.

Her eyes fell first on the Princess Cosmetics sign, then on the whole building, and she let out a horrified gasp.

"What?" Evan asked, alarmed.

"I clash!"

"What?"

"Look at me!" she said. "Why on earth did I wear red? I clash with the sign, the building, and everything else that's Princess pink!"

Evan tilted his head and let out a deep laugh. "Sweetheart," he told her softly, "no one dresses to match the product. Trust me. You look beautiful."

She slowly raised her eyes beneath guarded brows, feeling silly. "Are you sure?"

"More than sure."

As she stepped onto the crowded elevator with Evan a moment later, the ride to his office felt almost surreal to her. How on earth had she ended up here? It seemed impossible that this was really happening. No one looked twice at her, and it was almost as if she belonged there—in the elevator, in the building, in the business world itself.

And she began to think she might like this.

EVAN WENT THROUGH his morning mail, all the while thinking of Cassandra. She and Miriam had hit it off right away—he could tell that Miriam thought she was as sweet and wonderful as he did—and now they were busy at work. Cassandra had relayed all her ideas to Miriam and together they were structuring and outlining the presentation.

He noticed that they'd worked right through the lunch hour together, and soon he planned to break up the powwow and insist on treating them both to a late lunch someplace nice. Then maybe, if they had time before the end of the day, he would give Cassandra a tour of the building.

Reaching into his inbox for the last handful of mail, he discovered a small box wrapped in brown paper bearing a feminine scrawl. He opened it with curiosity and, to his surprise, found a new tie to replace the one that had been ruined by the spilled iced tea last week, by the nervous waitress in that little diner. The gesture both surprised and touched him. She'd not enclosed a note, but no one else could have sent it. He hated to think of her spending her hard earned money on him, but he still thought it a classy move.

Just then, Cassandra burst through his office door. "I'm so excited, Evan!"

Hearing those words from her lips was almost

enough to excite him, too, but he knew she was talking about business, so he tried not to think about his pants. He smiled up at her. "Is your work going well then?"

"It's going great," she said, beaming. "I feel really good about it."

"See, I told you things would be fine," he replied as she approached his desk.

"Well, I haven't given the presentation yet," she said a little skeptically, "but I'm feeling more prepared for it all the time."

He liked seeing that confident glint in her eye, and hmm...he couldn't help it—everything about her right now made him want her, and he had *no choice* but to think about his pants.

But knock it off. There's Miriam to think about, and lunch. Besides, Cassandra's presentation might save the company—he'd better let her concentrate on it.

Evan watched as her eyes fell on his cluttered desk. "Oh, it came," she said.

"What came?" It seemed almost as if she was looking at the tie.

She bit her lip and began to fidget with a button on her suit. "Um, your United Charities pledge card," she said—then began talking faster. "You know, I'd really appreciate it if you could earmark part of your contribution to the Sunshine House. They subsist almost entirely on private donations and it's not easy to make ends meet and run a decent shelter. Even small donations really count."

He'd forgotten about her concern for the homeless, but being reminded warmed his heart. "That's the place where you volunteer, right?"

She nodded.

"I'll be sure to write them a sizable check." Anything for the woman he loved. She was such a good soul. "Now," he said, "let's go get Miriam and have lunch."

THAT NIGHT CASSIE and Evan lay in bed, Evan reading the Wall Street Journal and Cassie studying her outline for tomorrow's presentation. But she let her mind wander, thinking not only about the day to come but also the day just past.

Working in the office with Miriam had been exhilarating—even better than Cassie had always imagined. She could hardly explain it, even to herself, but she'd come away invigorated and ready for more.

She glanced then at the new tie that lay on Evan's dresser. She'd almost blown it when she'd seen the tie lying on his desk. The tie that had started it all. Thank God she'd found a way to cover her blunder.

"Ready for tomorrow?" he asked, looking up from his paper.

She nodded. "I think so."

"Let's see what you've got." He leaned to peer over her shoulder at her notes.

"Well, first," she explained, perusing the outline Miriam had typed up for her, "I'll talk about the changing needs of women in today's society, how they want greater variety and less expense. I'll explain that we're fickle shoppers and that with everything there is on the market, we can afford to be. That's when I'll launch into the part about offering smaller quantities and maybe even sampler gift sets to be brought out initially at Christmastime, and I'll propose that if they do well, we should continue to sell them throughout the year.

"Next, I'll move onto bigger marketing issues. I'll propose that Princess create an entirely new line of cosmetics called Princess Now. They'll be packaged in flowery containers with splashy colors. They'll feature new eye and lip shades, bold and bright and fun, to appeal to women thirty and under. The Princess Now line won't be sold behind glass counters, but on open shelves in department stores, specialty stores, and chain boutiques. The price will be clearly marked on every item. The idea here is not to be elusive and untouchable—but to be a fun, accessible, but still classy product for a younger generation.

"For our traditional longtime customers we'll retain our current product line, rebranding it Classic Princess. Classic Princess will still be sold behind glass, but we'll vary sizes more, and we'll update our packaging to a slightly more modern shade of pink, with black accents and script—and we have several options for that to show the board. The overall look will still be elegant but more contemporary.

"Additionally, each display will have a price list clearly posted, and a price brochure that can be taken by the customer. That way someone can browse the product line and check our prices without dealing with a salesperson if they choose. The brochures, by the way, will be printed on parchment—helping to retain the elegance Princess is known for while also being more accessible and convenient for the customer.

"If the Princess Now line takes off, we may also want to consider launching sub-lines for each season, offering new colors each spring, summer, winter, and fall. This wouldn't have to be elaborate, just a handful of new colors to be billed as our spring line or our fall line. This will appeal to women with frequently changing tastes or women who like to be up on the latest trends.

"All this will also launch a new marketing campaign to make people aware of Princess Now and also remind them of Classic Princess as well. This will cost some money, of course, but it'll be worth it. The overarching idea will be that Princess Cosmetics offers something for every woman."

When she finished speaking, Evan just stared at her. He stayed so quiet for so long that she began to get nervous. "Well," she said, her heart rising to her throat, "don't keep me in suspense—what do you think?"

Evan looked a little stunned. Until finally he said, "I'm...thrilled."

Cassie's eyes widened on him. "Thrilled? Really?" That was more than she had even hoped for.

"Really," he said, nodding and smiling enthusiastically. "I just had no idea it would be so…far reaching. So…all-encompassing. So…so…"

"What?"

"So damn good, Cassandra."

A deep satisfaction bloomed in Cassie's heart. "You really think so? It's really good?"

Finally, now, Evan smiled, seeming to break free from his initial shock. "It's great, honey. No, it's *more* than great. It's just exactly what the doctor ordered to get this business moving again. I mean it. You're just what Princess needed."

Cassie simply beamed at him. This was all coming together in a way that felt almost serendipitous. And she wasn't nearly as nervous about her presentation tomorrow as she had been before. In fact, she was so proud of her ideas that a part of her was even looking forward to it.

"Listen, honey," Evan said then, taking her hands in his, "I want to ask you something."

Cassie stiffened. What could this be?

"We've discussed a lot that you're looking for the perfect job. And I know that right now Princess might not look too attractive to you, considering what I've told you about our…recent decline. But the place needs someone like you. You're proving that to me more and more. So…should the board approve your proposal or even any part of it, I want you to know that my number one choice for who should get the ball rolling would be you. I don't know if you're interested, but if you'd give

Princess a chance, I'd love to have you there."

Cassie just blinked. Had he just said what she thought he'd said? "Have me there? Like, to work there? Be employed there?"

"To spearhead this whole initiative," he said, being more specific.

"Spearhead," she repeated numbly.

"Yes, to work with our marketing department in getting all the changes in place after they're approved."

Cassie took all that in for a moment, absorbing it. And then she couldn't help herself—she threw her arms around Evan's neck.

"Does that mean you'll consider it?" he asked, laughing.

"I'll take the job," she told him.

"You will?"

She couldn't believe how surprised he sounded. "Of course. I can't imagine anything more wonderful than going to work at Princess Cosmetics during the day and coming home to you at night."

A broad smile unfurled on Evan's face just before he pulled her closer, delivering a kiss to her forehead.

"Just one thing, though," she added, pulling back enough to lift her eyes to his. It had just dawned on her. "What would happen if we...you know...broke up?"

"It wouldn't matter," he promised. "Marketing is on a whole different floor of the office, we wouldn't work that closely in the big picture, and we're both mature enough to handle it. But you may as well know...I'm not expecting that to happen."

His eyes filled with love as he looked at her, the kind of love she had only dreamed about until a week ago, and Cassie knew no more words were necessary right now. She lifted her lips softly to his, the connection with him raining tenderness and heat over her whole body.

Well, okay, maybe a *few* more words. "Make love to me," she whispered softly in his ear.

And he did.

THE NEXT DAY, when Miriam was preparing a conference room for the big presentation, Cassie made sure the coast was clear, then picked up the phone on Miriam's desk.

Looking down at the fitted black suit she wore, Cassie felt confident, authoritative, and professional. She liked where she was and wanted to stay here, which meant she should be concentrating on her presentation notes—but there was so much more on her mind.

"Fast Eddie's," Jewel answered.

"Jewel, it's me," Cassie said, keeping her voice low.

"Hey kid, how's it going in the corporate world?" Jewel sounded happy to hear from her.

"Um, better than expected, actually."

"Yeah? That's great. Tell me everything."

"I'd love to, but I can't right now—no time." Cassie paused to take a deep breath. "Although I do need to ask a huge favor."

Jewel hesitated and Cassie knew her favors were starting to run low. She spoke quickly. "It's like this, Jewel. Evan offered me a job at Princess. A big job. In marketing. I've accepted, but I'm not even sure I can do it. And so the thing is, I can't afford to quit Eddie's—not yet anyway. This whole thing could backfire and then where would I be? So…"

"Go ahead, Cass," Jewel said.

"If you could just cover for me the rest of the week— tell Eddie I'm stuck in Kentucky until Friday—I'll never ask you for anything again. By the time Monday morning rolls around this will all be over one way or the other, I promise. I'll make some kind of decision, because…well, I just have to. So if you can just do this for me for two more days, I'll be totally indebted to you for life."

Jewel sighed. "I don't want you to be indebted to me, kid—I just want you to be happy. So sure, two more days. I can handle it."

Cassie was flooded with relief. "Thanks Jewel! You're the best!"

"Listen, though," Jewel said, "there's some stuff going on here that you should know about."

The words caught Cassie off guard. "What?"

"Eddie may be selling the place."

"Selling the diner?" She couldn't believe it.

"Yeah. Says he wants to move to Florida, be near his parents during their last years."

"Wow," Cassie said.

"The prospective buyer is coming to look at the place before opening on Sunday morning," Jewel explained. "But Eddie says he's made an arrangement with the guy to keep our jobs safe."

"Well, that's a relief," Cassie replied.

"Thing is, Eddie needs somebody to come in after closing at midnight on Saturday and give the place a good cleaning before morning."

"Things always look pretty clean when we get there," Cassie pointed out.

"Yeah, but he's talking about the things that only get cleaned once in awhile. He wants to give the place a good once over, you know? And as it happens, I'm going out of town for the weekend with Malcolm."

Malcolm? With all the harried happenings in her life, Cassie had completely forgotten about Jewel's romance. She felt extremely remiss not to know what was going on in her friend's social life. "Wow, Jewel, that's wonderful!"

"Anyway," Jewel said, "Eddie can't get any of the other girls to work all night. But he *is* willing to pay double-time for it. So…"

It sounded like a grim task, and Cassie had no idea what she'd tell Evan, but she knew she owed it to Jewel, and to Eddie. The pay didn't even matter. "Tell Eddie he can count on me to do it," Cassie said.

STANDING OUTSIDE THE conference room door, Evan couldn't take his eyes off Cassandra in that black suit.

He'd seen plenty of black suits on plenty of women before, yet none compared to this. But he couldn't let himself think about that right now. The future of Princess Cosmetics hung in the balance.

"Are you ready?" he asked her. The board waited inside.

Cassandra nodded, and he reached for the doorknob. Only then he stopped—because the hints of guilt that had nagged at him for days were suddenly eating a hole through his stomach. How had he been so dishonest with her? How had he *stayed* so dishonest with her? "I can't do it," he said.

Her pretty eyes went wide on him. "Can't do what?"

"I can't let you go in there without telling you the whole truth."

He hated the strange look that grew on her face, but forged ahead.

"Cassandra, I...haven't been completely honest."

Chapter Twelve

―❦―

"**W**HAT?" SHE MURMURED.

Evan took a deep breath and summoned his courage. "I hardly know where the hell to begin."

"Well, find a place," she urged him.

Given the not particularly great time he'd chosen to do this—without a plan no less—he decided to just say it all as quickly as he could, the consequences be damned. It was the only way. "Cassandra, Princess's problems are more than slight and they're more than just this quarter. We're on our last leg. And those acquisitions? They were desperate moves on my part to start raking in some revenue." He sighed. "I wanted to tell you, I really did. But…"

"But what, Evan?" she asked softly.

He lowered his eyes, unable to look at her right now. "I guess I…didn't want to give you a bad impression. I suppose I was afraid you might…think less of me."

"Evan," she began, but he cut her off.

"My lame excuses aren't important, though. What's important is that I couldn't let you go before the board without telling you. And what's even more important is that I couldn't let you take a job with my company without knowing the truth, either.

"I won't hold you to what you said last night in bed, accepting the job. I'd fudged the truth to you about the company so much that I guess I almost started believing myself that things weren't so bad. But they are. And I would never jeopardize your career opportunities by asking you to work for a failing company."

He paused. "So there you have it. The ugly truth. I'm sorry I wasn't honest with you sooner. And I hope you don't hate me."

When Evan quit speaking, his heart raced a mile a minute. He was seldom dishonest and he could scarcely believe he'd been that way with her of all people, the woman he wanted a future with. And now he'd just laid everything on the line.

Cassandra looked up at him with narrowed, stricken eyes. He peered down at her and hoped she could somehow feel the enormity of his regret and find it in her heart to forgive him.

"I don't hate you," she finally said. "I could *never* hate you. I love you."

He *whoosh*ed out a heavy sigh as relief washed over him. "You don't know what that means to me."

Then she took a deep breath. "And I forgive you for not being totally forthcoming with me."

"Really?"

"The things you held back weren't significant," she

said. "Not really. Not in the big scheme of things. And...well, I know how hard it can be to tell the truth sometimes."

"So you're not mad at me? Not even a little?"

She shook her head. "Not even a little. In fact," she added, "I guess I feel...really important now. To know you would choose *me* to make a presentation that's so...momentous."

"It *is* momentous. But still, I meant what I said, honey. I don't expect you to take the job I offered you."

"But I want to," she said easily.

And Evan could hardly believe his ears. "You do? Even now, knowing what you know?"

"Yes. I mean...if you still want me to when this is all over."

"When what's all over?"

She shook her head then, seeming suddenly nervous. "My presentation."

"Why *wouldn't* I want you to take the job?"

She sighed, now looking more troubled than he could easily make sense of. "No reason, I guess."

She appeared unsettled enough that he went so far as to place his hand on her elbow. "Are you okay, Cassandra?"

"Fine," she said with a strained smile. "Really. I'm just a little nervous about...you know, going in there."

"Maybe because I just made it seem a lot more important," he realized aloud, feeling bad about that. She was amazing for forgiving him so easily, but his timing had sure as hell lacked finesse.

"Maybe," she said quietly, still looking tense.

They both glanced toward the conference room door.

"They're waiting," Evan said. "And I know you'll do a great job. Don't let what I just told you change anything about how you view this. No matter how it turns out, your proposal is fantastic and you're going to go far in the business world."

Cassandra took a deep breath and he could tell his words had heartened her. "I'm ready," she said. "And I meant what I said, Evan. I admire your honesty more than you know."

Evan leaned in to kiss her cheek. Then he reached down and opened the door.

EVAN SAT DOWN at the end of the long mahogany table and waited. Cassandra looked gorgeous as she rose from her seat and walked to the front of the room toward the overhead projector. "Good afternoon, gentlemen," she said. Her voice sounded cool and confident and betrayed not even a hint of nervousness. His stomach tingled.

He watched in admiration as she discussed the changing needs of today's busy woman, speaking clearly and simply, her tone exuding comfort and sureness. He noticed right away how the old men on the Princess board tuned in to her—by her third sentence she had them in the palm of her hand. He'd known she would do well, but he still couldn't help being impressed.

As he continued to observe her, the way she moved and talked, the way she smiled and made eye contact with the board members, his mind drifted away from her words while his senses honed in on her body and the way she used it to move around the room, poising her hand on the table before her or taking confident steps on those long, pretty legs. He was surprised when he felt a prickle of arousal between his *own* legs. But not *completely* surprised. Everything she did turned him on.

She held the room in her grasp—every eye rested upon her. Evan found it hard to believe she'd been so nervous about this—she'd become an arresting and powerful presence in the room. Her sense of authority combined with her incredible femininity to make Evan's arousal grow to peak stiffness when she drew her eyes from the board members to meet his, only for a second, but what an electrifying second it was. He wondered how he could survive the rest of her presentation.

The minutes dragged on and he reminded himself that he had more important things to think about than sex. Like the fact that he'd finally been honest with Cassandra and she'd forgiven him completely. And like his company, the company his parents had built together and made into a cosmetics empire. Cassandra's talk this afternoon might very well provide the impetus that would save it—and yet all he could think about was getting under her sexy skirt.

CASSIE SAT IN the big leather chair behind Evan's desk. He'd be in the board meeting for at least a few more minutes while she waited in his office.

She thought about his lie. Which, as she'd told him, was nothing in the big scheme of things. She remembered the look in his eyes as he'd spewed it all out to her, and she imagined the time he'd spent worrying and toiling over it. She hoped he hadn't wasted too much energy on worry, especially now that she knew how much else had been weighing on his mind, too, like the future of his company. Still, it made her respect him all the more to know he considered his omissions about Princess's financial situation to be so serious.

Then she thought about *her* lie. Now *that* was a lie. In fact, it was lots and lots of lies, all summed, probably more than Evan had told in his entire life. His admission of guilt outside the conference room might have prompted her own, but the timing had been terrible. It would have been impossible. Even if it made her feel all the more guilty now.

Stop it—this is no time to feel sad.

After all, she was wearing a gorgeous suit, she'd just made a killer presentation, and Evan Hunt was in love with her. And when she thought about all those things at once, it made her downright giddy—enough that she spun the chair in a circle. She was in love, the world was beautiful, and nothing was going to spoil her happiness.

She smiled to herself. Evan had worn the tie today. She'd noticed it first thing this morning, but during her presentation her eyes had been continually drawn to it. To *him.*

When she'd bought that tie and sat alone in her apartment touching it so ridiculously, she'd thought she'd never get to touch *it,* or *him,* again. It had been like a last desperate grab at the desire she'd felt for him that first day in the diner. Now she could touch the tie, and the man who wore it, as often as she wanted, everywhere. She bit her lip, a tickle of passion edging its way up her inner thighs.

She couldn't believe how well the presentation had gone. Once she'd taken the floor, speaking to the board had felt like the most natural thing in the world, like something she'd been born to do. She smiled again, remembering how comfortable and smart she'd felt before them, how much a part of the company she seemed to become in the half hour she spoke.

Evan's eyes on her had been incredible, full of light and passion and hope. She'd tried not to look at him, lest she get distracted, but the tie had continued to draw her gaze back to the man behind it. *Her* man. Her lover. She shivered with the knowledge.

Thinking of the tie, Cassie began to realize that she was surrounded yet again by all that was him, his possessions. But this was different than at home. Here, it was the leather chair beneath her—he sat here all day, she thought. It was the things on his desk—a small paperweight shaped like a globe, another bearing his initials. She reached for it and ran her fingertips over the letters. It was the ink pens he wrote with, the notes he had scrawled.

Her stomach jolted when her eyes fell on a tiny piece of paper with her name and address scribbled on it. Behind the name *Cassandra* were three exclamation points. She pictured him doodling them while speaking with her on the phone. They meant *excitement, excitement, excitement.* That's how much she excited him. It turned her on to know that he'd wanted her that much, even then, when they'd barely known each other. She wished she could excite him right now.

Rising from the desk, she walked to the big plate glass window that looked out over the city, taking in the magnificent view. *You've come a long way, baby. You're taking Chicago by storm!*

When the office door clicked open, Cassie turned. And Evan's smile nearly took her breath away as he quickly crossed the floor to where she stood.

"Well?" she asked, her eyebrows rising.

"You were fabulous!"

"But did they like me?"

"They were extremely impressed," he replied.

Cassie trembled from all the emotions inside her. "Did they vote yet?"

"No," Evan said, "Not yet. It's customary for changes this big that they take time to mull it over for a couple of days. But I feel good about it, honey. *Really* good."

As she turned back to enjoy the view, Evan closed the gap between them, wrapping his arms around her from behind as she leaned back against his chest. They stayed silent for a moment as Cassie tried to catch her breath from all that had happened over the past two days. But it was hard to relax when she found herself wanting to attack him. The tickle of desire snaking up her legs earlier had turned to a full blown pulsing inside her panties.

"What are you thinking?" Evan asked her.

"Beautiful view," she lied.

He moved around in front of her then, blocking the window. "I've got the most beautiful view in the city right now," he said, gazing into her eyes. He lifted his hand to trace the line of her jaw with one feathery fingertip, then trailed down her neck to end at the V of her suit jacket that stopped just above her breasts.

She took in the heat growing in Evan's emerald gaze—just before he pressed his body against her, his hands closing firmly over her hips, and his stiffness melded with the cleft between her legs. A tremor passed through her from head to toe. Apparently, she wasn't the only one who was turned on.

"Do you know what you did to me just now?" he whispered, the warmth of his breath kissing her ear. "Do you know how aroused I got just watching you make that presentation? Do you have any idea how sexy you are, how hot you look in that suit?"

Cassie could barely breathe beneath the weight of his

sensual words. And in a voice that came out raspy from her own desire, she replied, "I'd rather let you look at me out of it."

Evan wasted no time taking advantage of Cassandra's offer. He worked to unbutton her jacket, then watched as she shrugged it to the floor. He took the cups of her lacy black bra into his hands as he kissed her neck and her throat, turning to lean her back against the glass.

"Evan," she whispered, "what if someone sees?"

He glanced over her shoulder out the huge window as he nudged his leg between hers. "We're fifty stories high," he said. "It doesn't matter."

His hands found her thighs then, gliding over her smooth skin to push her short skirt up, stopping at her hips. He shifted his hands to her ass, drawing her close as she began to move against him. His breath came hot and uncontrolled in her ear. "I want to do everything to you," he whispered throatily. Then slid one hand to the silk between her legs.

Her labored sigh fueled him and he couldn't wait another minute. Frantically, he reached for the zipper on the back of her skirt, soon shoving it, along with her panties, to the floor, helping her step out of both. Again he pushed her back against the glass, using his hands to free her breasts from the cups of her bra, soon licking wildly at her beautiful, taut nipples. The hardness against his tongue only added to his intense need. "I have to have you," he breathed.

He watched her face, her eyes glazed with passion as

she worked with his belt and zipper. Finally she freed him and he pressed himself hot against her naked belly. "Do you want me inside you?" he rasped.

Her lips trembled. "God, yes, Evan."

Evan lifted one of her legs and she wrapped it around his waist. The pointed heel of her shoe dug into his ass, taking away his last remnants of self-control. He thrust into her then, fast and deep, burying himself in her warmth. He ran his hands over her arms and breasts, her hips and thighs. Raining heated kisses over her lips and her neck, he soon lowered them to her shoulders and then her breasts, all the while pumping furiously into her welcoming body. He loved the way she responded, meeting each stroke with eager movements of her own.

"Let me sit on top of you," she whispered up to him.

"Oh baby," he breathed. Then he picked her up, both her legs wrapping around him, and he carried her to the big leather chair behind the desk. Lowering himself down into it left her already situated on top of him. She straddled him, her knees sinking into the leather on both sides of his body.

Cassie had never experienced such wild bliss as she did gyrating against Evan in his chair. She felt beautiful and sexy and alive in his arms. His hands gripped her bottom as he pushed himself deeper into her, forcing a low moan from her throat. "Oh God, Evan," she breathed—and a familiar sensation began to build inside her, like a spark that bursts into a flame. "Oh God," she breathed again, moving in tiny circles on him that grew tighter and hotter with each passing second.

And then it happened, the sweet hot release exploding inside her like a thousand flashes of light, blinding her, burying her, moving her through heaven at an incredible speed, until finally the pulsing waned and she fell against him in the chair, needing to be held very tight—which he did without being asked, while he whispered sweet words in her ear.

"I love you. You're so beautiful."

The deeply whispered words mixed with the beating of her heart as she clung to him, wishing, hoping, praying that everything would be all right. She had to find a way to tell him the truth—she simply had to. She loved him too much to keep living a lie.

When she lifted her head from his shoulder and looked into his sparking eyes, she was surprised at the depth of emotion she found there. "I want to be like this with you forever," he whispered.

Cassie drew in her breath and her heart began to hurt with love and pain and confusion, and the passion that was already growing inside her again. "I want that, too," she promised him.

Then he slowly resumed his movement inside her, filling her with himself, with his love. She looked into his eyes, no longer embarrassed to let him see all the desire that rested there, and their gazes locked.

Soon his thrusts were lifting her up, but he used his hands to pull her hips down on him, burying his hardness in her as deep as possible. She began to cry out with each incredible jolt, but then remembered where they were and reached up a hand to cover her mouth.

"I sent Miriam home early," he whispered knowingly. "We're all alone."

Oh, that was good news—because the moans and shrieks that left her came from a place so deep they could scarcely be controlled. She no longer tried to quiet them, but let herself cry out at each powerful stroke that filled her.

She continued to gaze into Evan's eyes, thinking she could drown there. Then his hard, deep thrusts started coming faster as he repeatedly pressed her body down to meet his. She heard herself panting, her heart beating wildly in her chest. She found herself moving against him again harder than before, arching her back and thrusting her breasts forward.

"Oh Evan," she cried, shocked that it was happening again, that those satiating waves were flowing over her once more, this time softer and sweeter, their departure leaving her completely spent.

Evan moaned beneath her then, almost growling his pleasure, and she knew it was happening for him too, so she moved on him hard, *helping* it happen, until finally he went still and pulled her to him in a tight embrace.

They stayed quiet until finally he whispered, "Are you okay?"

"Okay?" she murmured in reply. "I'm more than okay. I didn't know it could happen twice."

He laughed into her neck, nuzzling her. "Next time

we'll go for three."

As Cassie lifted her head to look around the office, she couldn't believe what they'd done there. She must've looked sheepish. "What's wrong?" Evan asked her.

"Nothing," she replied. "It's just that I've never done anything like this before."

And he smiled. "Neither have I."

Chapter Thirteen

O N FRIDAY AFTERNOON, Cassie sat on the couch in Evan's office. She played with color swatches from the art department, the same she'd shared with the board. Evan had wanted her to dive right into it, feeling confident her plans would be approved.

I can do this. Never mind that I don't have the first clue about marketing. And never mind that Evan doesn't need a new employee in a position they aren't qualified for. She'd come this far, she could surely continue. It would simply take a lot of hard work, dedication, and focus.

Unfortunately, Cassie had even more important things on her mind than the marketing of Princess Cosmetics. Not the least of which was the annual shareholder's banquet tonight at a fancy downtown hotel. As usual, she had nothing to wear. In fact, she'd hung onto her borrowed suits for two extra days— managing to alter their looks with accessories—and as of this afternoon, she would have nothing to wear to work at Princess next week either. She already felt naked.

She looked up to find Evan smiling at her from behind his desk. "What?" she asked, feeling scrutinized.

"Nothing," he laughed. "I just like having you here. It's gonna be a bummer when we actually have to get you your own office."

Her own office? Cassie still couldn't get used to any of this. It had all happened so fast. "Only if the board approves my proposal," she reminded him.

"Like I told you," he said, "there's a position for you here no matter what happens with the board."

Elation and shame warred within her at his words. He was simply too good to her. If he only knew the lying, conniving girl she really was…

"You know what?" he said with a tilt of his head. "I'm actually looking forward to tonight. I usually hate these mandatory galas, but with you on my arm I expect it to be a lot more fun than usual."

She returned his smile, wondering if she could possibly talk Irma into one more loaner—a dress for tonight.

"What are you wearing?" he asked then, as if reading her mind.

"I'm not sure yet. I may have to…do some last-minute shopping."

Without hesitation, he reached into his jacket and pulled out a credit card. "Go buy yourself a gorgeous dress," he said, offering her the plastic.

"Evan," she said, stunned at his generosity, "you don't have to—"

"I know I don't have to," he cut her off. "I *want* to. I want to give you a gift for all the work you've done for me this week. And…maybe for also forgiving me so easily. And…because I love you. See how deserving you are?"

Cassie rose from her sofa and reluctantly took the card from Evan's fingers. The last thing she wanted to do was take advantage of him. *But what am I thinking? I've been taking advantage of him since day one.* She sighed. *So then, heck, why not buy the dress, too?* Besides, she really didn't want to ask Irma for another favor, so this would solve at least one problem. And she resolved to pay him back as soon as she could.

When Evan glanced at the clock on his desk, her eyes were drawn there, as well. A little after two. "Why don't you take the rest of the day and go buy that dress," he suggested. "I can meet you at home later."

Cassie quickly took him up on the offer. Not that she didn't love her new job, but everything hinged on the coming weekend. She had big decisions to make and financial problems to solve. Plus she had to work at Eddie's late Saturday night—as if she didn't have enough to keep her busy these days. Taking the afternoon for herself sounded more than appealing.

The first stop she made was at Fast Eddie's Diner. "Where's Eddie?" Cassie whispered when she walked into the mid-afternoon quiet of the place and found Jewel rolling forks and knives into napkins. She didn't necessarily want Eddie to see her in her black suit since he'd probably assume it was funeral wear and she'd have to start feeling guilty for *that* all over again.

"Meeting with his real estate agent," Jewel said. Then she raised her eyes and gave Cassie a once-over. "Whoa! Look at you! You look fabulous, kid!"

"Thanks," Cassie said with a smile.

"You look like a marketing professional already."

"Good, because I think I'm going to keep it. I'm on my way to return the red suit to Irma right now, but I'm going to use my pay check to buy this one. And speaking of my check, where is it?"

Jewel reached beneath the counter. "I hid it under the lost and found bin."

Cassie peeked casually around the counter and caught sight of the silly pink mask she'd worn when Evan had come in. She shook her head in disgust. Everywhere she went, reminders of her lies taunted her.

As Jewel handed Cassie her check, she said, "So, you're starting your business wardrobe, huh?"

Cassie nodded tentatively. "I'm not sure what I'll wear to work the other four days of next week," she said. "And I don't know how I'm going to pay my rent, either—this is money I would usually tuck away for that. But I've got to start somewhere, right?"

Jewel's smile was half-hearted and consoling. They both knew what it was like to be stretched thin financially. "Sit down, Cass," she said, leading her to one of the booths. "Tell me everything I've missed."

Cassie filled Jewel in on the past days as best she could. Although so much had happened in such a short period of time that her mind could barely retain it all.

She ended with, "So, we've got this big Princess bash tonight and I'm stooping so low as to let Evan buy me a dress, and I'm financially and emotionally distressed, and I'm not sure how much longer I can keep pulling this off, and…well, like I told you, by the time this weekend is over, my immediate future will have been decided one way or the other."

"What do you mean?" Jewel asked. "One way or the other."

"Well, I'll either find the guts to tell him, at which point he'll ship me back to my apartment and I'll be returning this suit and reporting to work here bright and early Monday morning in telltale pink, or I'll convince myself that I can live with my lies, start learning the ropes of the corporate world, and continue being with the man I love."

But to her surprise, Jewel's gaze shone with concern. "Would you listen to yourself? Trying to convince yourself you can live a lie? Indefinitely? Are you serious, Cass?"

Cassie huffed out a breath, feeling defensive. "Hey, since when don't you condone lying?"

"Since I see what it's done to you," Jewel said matter-of-factly. "Some of us can live on the reckless side and some of us can't. Apparently, you fall into the 'can't' category. I mean, look at you. You're an emotional wreck and this situation has gotten way out of hand."

Cassie sighed. "It's far from ideal, I know."

"Far from ideal? It sucks."

She knew that was entirely true—but she was dealing with it as best she could. "Just give me the weekend, Jewel. I'll work it out. I'll make a decision. I'll figure out what will be the best for everyone in the end. I will."

To her shame, though, Cassie had a feeling that she might ultimately decide on the path that Jewel had suddenly turned against—trying to live with her lie. She loved Evan too much to willingly let him go. And telling him the truth would be equivalent to throwing him away because she knew the result would be the same.

Eventually, of course, as their relationship developed, there would be more questions that needed answers—about Harvard, about Atlanta, and who knew what else. But she would figure it all out somehow—the same way she had so far.

She rose from the booth quickly, anxious to escape the worry she saw in Jewel's eyes.

"Thanks for everything, Jewel," Cassie said. "I'll call you by Sunday night to let you know what's happening."

"Wait," Jewel said before she could leave. Then her friend walked over to the counter and returned a few seconds later carrying the pink cat mask. She stuffed it down into Cassie's purse. "I think you should take this with you."

"Why on earth should I do that?"

"To remind you," Jewel said, "that you can't go through life wearing a mask."

CASSIE FELT BOTH beautiful and on edge walking into the lavish hotel on Evan's gallant arm. He looked handsome in his classic black tux, and she wore a simple but elegant sheath of black that conformed to her shape. She'd charged some sophisticated-looking jewelry to complete her elegant look, and her hair was swept up into a fancy up-do, just like on the night when she'd first become Cassandra.

"Don't be surprised if you're the center of attention tonight," he told her softly as they approached the banquet room.

She turned to him, more than a little surprised. "Me? Why?"

"Well, let's just say my associates aren't used to seeing me with a woman on my arm. I haven't dated anyone seriously for a couple of years—I've been too wrapped up in saving Princess. Until now. And besides," he added with a wink, "why *wouldn't* you be the center of attention? You'll be the most gorgeous woman in the room."

Cassie blushed beneath her Princess makeup and Evan grinned down at her. Just one look from his green eyes made her blood race—how on earth could she be expected to give that up by telling him the truth?

Entering the extravagant dinner on Evan's arm was another surreal moment. Was this really her, Cassie Turner from Hargrove, Kentucky? All dressed up and with the most handsome man in the room? Preparing to hobnob with top executives and key decision makers?

"Cassandra Turner," Evan introduced her to first one person and then the next, "Princess's newest associate."

But Cassie could tell as she smiled and shook hands that it was clear that she was more than an associate to Evan. People cast smiles in her direction, their eyes expressing approval. One guy, whom Cassie remembered from the cat mask fiasco at the diner, even said, "Nice to see you out with a beautiful young lady this evening, Evan."

It felt wonderful to know they all thought her worthy of him, to know they thought she was one of them.

Maybe she was.

During the delectable dinner, Cassie sat next to Evan joining in on conversation when appropriate, smiling and laughing, being his Cassandra. She felt both triumphant...and false. And as she laughed at a joke from across the table, she wished she could *forget* the false part, just wipe it out of her mind for good.

She excused herself to the restroom before dessert was served, and stood before the mirror floofing her bangs when another woman joined her to re-apply lipstick from a Princess pink tube. "Hi, I'm Diana Kramer," she said with a smile. "I work in accounting."

"Cassandra Turner," she replied.

"You're here with Evan Hunt, aren't you?"

"Um, yes, I am."

"Lucky girl," Diana said. "Mr. Hunt is a real catch, don't you think?"

What to say? She decided on, "Evan's a wonderful

man."

Like so many others, Diana Kramer smiled in that knowing way—she, too, must have been privy to Evan's recent lack of a love life. "Hope you enjoy the evening," Diana said, starting to depart.

"Maybe I'll see you around the office," Cassie offered on a lark.

"Oh?" Diana tilted her head to the side.

"Yes, I'm going to be working in marketing."

Diana tilted her head, clearly curious. "I had no idea. What will you be doing?"

Yikes, what had she started here? "Well," she began tentatively, "nothing's firmly in place yet, but it's likely I may be...overseeing some new company branding."

"Oh, congratulations!" Diana said, her eyes gone wide. "I hope you won't mind my saying, but you look awfully young for that kind of position. You must have a heck of a background to land that job. Where'd you go to school?"

Of course, now Cassie wanted to lie down and die. "Harvard," she calmly replied. No, she wanted to slither out the door like the snake she was.

"No kidding. Me, too!"

Cassie held in her gasp of horror. "Wow," she said, trying to force a smile. "Small world."

"Don't you miss it? All the ivy, all the history?"

"All the time."

"Where did you live?"

"Huh?"

"In the dorms or off campus? What part of town? I was in Central Square."

Oh Lord. "I...uh...moved around a lot while I was there."

"Listen, we should get together soon and—"

"You know," Cassie cut her off, "I hate to chat and run, but I told Evan I'd be back in a jiffy, and my jiffy is up. He'll think I fell in. Sorry. Nice to meet you."

And she was out the door, her heart pounding mercilessly. And her guilt scale rising to the top. Now not only was she lying, but she was being rude to nice people, too. Where on earth would this end?

Despite what she'd told Diana Kramer, she simply couldn't go back to Evan just yet. She needed some air, a minute to regroup. So instead of heading toward the banquet room, she rushed through the plush lobby and stepped out onto the sidewalk that lined Wacker Drive.

"Cassie?"

She blinked, caught off guard by the voice, then looked up to find Mac ambling toward her on the sidewalk.

"Mac—hi," she said. She tried to smile at him, but her heart instantly broke. Here she was, in a semi-formal dress, eating a ridiculously expensive meal, and there was Mac, wearing the only set of clothes she'd ever seen him in, looking hungry and slightly sad. His face seemed gaunt, his eyes looming larger than usual.

"Look at you," Mac said appreciatively. "Take it your out for some fancy night with your new beau?"

Cassie nodded, suddenly not thinking at all about Evan. For the first time, it dawned on her that she hadn't been to the diner since Monday, and who knew if Jewel had remembered to give Mac anything to eat? It horrified her to realize how terribly selfish she'd become, how much she'd started neglecting the things she cared about. How could she have let that happen when she knew she'd become a key part of Mac's day-to-day life?

"Have you been eating?" she asked him.

"A little."

Cassie's heart flooded with grief. "I'm so sorry, Mac. I haven't been into work all week. I guess Jewel didn't remember?"

"On Tuesday and Wednesday she did. I didn't see her after that, though, so I guess she forgot."

She pressed splayed fingers to her chest. "Oh, Mac, I'm sorry!"

"That's all right, Cassie. I got by."

"Stay right here," she told him.

"What?"

"I'm in there eating a meal fit for a king, and there's no reason why I can't share it," she said. Then she rushed in off the street, back through the lobby. She sneaked furtively back into the banquet room, glad that Evan's back faced her and that he sat halfway across the room. Locating a waiter's table filled with half-eaten plates of food, she turned her back to the crowd, took one plate, and gathered as much as she could onto it. Chunks of chicken, remnants of the vegetable medley, a pile of new potatoes, and even an entire dinner roll.

She was about to make a dash back for the door when she spotted the desert cart nearby, packed with slabs of cake and pie. Mac would love that. She rose casually strolled to the cart, her heaping plate in hand. She picked up a large piece of chocolate cake, balancing it atop the plate, then for good measure she grabbed a piece of pecan pie, too. Last but not least, she thought, a fork and a napkin. No reason for Mac to have to eat like a slob.

Delicately balancing the mountain of food in her arms, she walked toward the dining room door, still unnoticed by Evan. Soon, he really *would* think she'd fallen in. She walked briskly across the lobby and back out onto the sidewalk, where Mac waited patiently.

His eyes grew wide when he saw the feast she carried. "Good Lord, Cassie," he said. "All that's for me?"

"What? Don't think you can eat it all?" she teased him.

"Oh, don't worry," he said, "I'll eat it. And I'll start with that chocolate cake." He lifted the dessert plate off the pile of leftover food and took the fork from Cassie's fingers. He settled on the sidewalk, leaning his back against the brick wall, and Cassie joined him, not even thinking about her dress.

She and Mac talked and laughed while he ate, and he only scolded her once for not having yet told Evan the truth about herself. Watching him eat, she felt thankful she'd roamed outside when she did.

She looked up from her spot on the sidewalk just in time to see Evan come out the front door of the hotel. Suddenly remembering why she was there, she knew she'd lingered too long. "There's Evan," she said to Mac, pointing him out. "I have to go."

Mac smiled at her and grabbed her hand before she could get up. Their eyes met. "Thanks, Cassie," he said.

"Cassandra?" Evan called.

Too late—he'd spotted her. She rose to greet him as he approached. "Sorry I wandered off," she apologized.

"I was getting worried," he said. And as he glanced down at the man on the sidewalk, Cassie thought it looked like Evan might *still* be worried.

"Evan," she began, "this is Mac. Mac is a friend of mine from the Sunshine House."

As the old man lifted his fork in way of greeting, Evan quickly figured out the situation. Cassandra had gathered up every leftover she could get her hands on and brought it out to this hungry, homeless man. "Nice to meet you, Mac," he said, extending his hand.

Mac set his fork on the dinner plate with a clatter and lifted his dirty hand. Evan shook it, thinking Cassandra was an angel.

"Well, Mac," she said, "enjoy your dinner, and I'll see you soon."

The man spoke with his mouth full of chocolate cake. "Thanks again, Cass...andra."

Evan took Cassandra's hand and led her back into the hotel lobby, after which she peered up at him sheepishly. "Sorry, Evan," she said. "But when I saw him out there looking so hungry, I had to do something. I hope this doesn't embarrass you too badly."

Wow—had he ever even known anyone this amazing? This giving? He wanted to crush her against him in a huge bear hug, but he knew it wasn't the time or the place. So instead he just gazed down into her beautiful, innocent eyes. "Honey," he began, "I think that's about the nicest gesture I've ever seen anyone make."

"Well, it's not just nice," she said, sounding almost self-deprecating. "Mac is my friend and he depends on me to help keep him fed. I don't think he's eaten in a couple of days. Evan, I've *got* to start spending time at the shelter again. I haven't been there since I met you, because...well, okay—I've been completely consumed with you. But that was so selfish of me—I didn't even think about people like Mac who need my help and count on me."

Evan was bowled over by her concern and generosity. He'd never met anyone who really helped those who were less fortunate. Oh sure, they all went to the fundraisers and gave to the charities, but seeing Cassandra sitting beside Mac on that sidewalk had touched him deeply. "I really admire you for that giving attitude," he said. "And I think you should spend as much time at the shelter as you want. And maybe," he added, "if you'd like, I could come with you."

Her eyes lit with fresh joy. "Would you, Evan? That would be wonderful. There are never enough hands. And these people have it so rough. Most of them really want to get back on their feet, but it's so hard for a homeless person to find a job without clean clothes or even an address to write down on an application. Mac, for instance. He's a dependable guy and he does his fair share around the shelter, too. But he can't even get a job at a fast food restaurant because he doesn't have clean clothes or a place to wash up on a daily basis. He has nothing of his own and it's like the world just wants to forget about him."

Evan was so moved by her concern that he wished there was some way he could make a difference. "You know," he ventured, "I could probably find your friend a job if you really think he'd be dependable."

Her eyes went as big and round as he'd ever seen them. "Oh, I know he would."

"It wouldn't be anything fancy. Just a janitor's job or something."

Cassandra beamed at him. "I'm sure Mac would like that fine. And just think, he could start saving some money, and maybe get a place of his own and—my goodness, he could live like a normal person again." She threw her arms around Evan's neck right there in the lobby of the hotel. "I'm sure this probably doesn't seem very professional, Evan," she said in his ear, "but I can't help it. Thank you so much for offering to help Mac! You don't know how happy that makes me."

"Anything for you, love," he said, taking in more of the beauty in her sparkling eyes. "Now, let's get back to the party. We're missing dessert. And besides, I have a surprise for you."

"A surprise?" She smiled up at him, clutching his arm as he led her back into the banquet room. "What kind of surprise?"

He couldn't resist teasing her. "If I told you, then it wouldn't be a surprise, would it? You'll find out after dessert."

Returning to their table, Cassie gobbled down a slice of rich chocolate cake, her stomach churning with anticipation. Part of her was still reeling over the developments with Mac and Evan since this had been an incredible night already—but now she was dying to find out Evan's surprise. Setting down her fork after shoveling the last bite of cake into her mouth, she stared at him expectantly.

"Impatience is not a virtue," he playfully informed her.

"Then tell me my surprise and I won't have to be impatient anymore."

"All right, all right," he conceded. "I was going to let you hear it when I present the company's one-year outlook in a few minutes, but I'll go ahead and tell you." He smiled widely. "The board met late this afternoon. And they approved each and every one of your proposed ideas. We're ready to move full steam ahead, honey."

For a second, Cassie couldn't catch her breath. This made it official—this was most perfect night ever. Even more than the night she'd met Evan. She couldn't believe it. She really *did* have a head for business! She felt proud and excited, and when Evan looked into her eyes with such unbridled appreciation, she simply felt...valued.

"There you are!"

Cassie looked up to find that Diana Kramer had already tracked her down, successfully interrupting one of the most important moments of her life. "Hi," Cassie greeted her.

"Hello, Diana," Evan said. "Do you two know each other?"

"We met in the bathroom," Cassie explained.

"And I discovered that Cassandra went to Harvard, too," Diana added, dropping into a vacant chair next to Cassie.

"That's right," Evan said. "You're a Harvard graduate yourself, aren't you?"

Diana nodded. "And I'm dying to spend some time with Cassandra now that I know she's a fellow alum. We should go shopping," she said, looking to Cassie.

"Um, sure, why not," Cassie replied.

"Don't you miss shopping in Harvard Square?" Diana asked her.

"Oh...yeah. Definitely."

"What was your favorite shop there?" Diana asked.

Geez—here we go again. And this time in front of Evan, too. "You know...to tell you the truth, I never had much time for shopping."

"Always hitting the books, I bet," Evan guessed.

"Say, who was your professor for Advanced Business

Law?" Diana asked out of nowhere.

Cassie closed her eyes and searched for an answer, some way out of this. And then she heard someone tapping on the microphone. A member of the board of directors had taken the podium and was calling the meeting portion of the evening to order. But she was beginning to wonder how much longer her luck could last.

"We'll chat later," Diana said, rising to go.

Cassie nodded forlornly and took a deep breath as Diana departed. *One more bullet dodged. But for how long?*

Beneath the table, Evan squeezed her hand and she smiled over at him, hoping he wouldn't realize how the effort suddenly strained her. A minute ago, she'd felt on top of the world. But now it suddenly felt like too much was happening too fast.

"I'D LIKE TO thank everyone for coming tonight, employees and shareholders alike," Evan said into a microphone a few minutes later. "And the first thing I want to tell you is that Princess Cosmetics will be undergoing a major facelift in the coming months. This has nothing to do with how our company is run, but everything to do with how our products are conceived, packaged, and delivered to the public. These exciting changes come at a time when Princess needs them, and they're the brainchild of our newest associate, Cassandra

Turner. Cassandra, please stand up for a moment."

With her stomach doing cartwheels, Cassie barely found the strength to rise from her chair. But she somehow managed it, turning to face the source of the mild applause that filled the room.

"Ms. Turner is a graduate of Harvard Business School and our board of directors will agree with me when I tell you that her innovative ideas are just what Princess needs to get back on its feet."

Evan kept talking, but Cassie sank slowly back down into her seat. She was on an emotional rollercoaster and, at the moment, it was headed straight down. She heard Evan speaking about Princess Now and Classic Princess, but the words began to run together. She felt as if a freight train barreled through her head.

Sure, the new job was great—it was all Cassie had ever wanted and she was proud of her innovations. But all these lies. They were everywhere. Coming from every direction, bouncing off all the people she'd told them to only to land right back in her face! And it wasn't just Evan, either. It was Eddie, and it was Diana Kramer. It was Miriam. Now it was this entire room full of people. God, next she'd probably start lying to Mac and Jewel.

No. No, no, no.

She wanted to lay her head down on the table and cry. She wanted to throw up her hands and surrender everything. As those grueling moments passed, she realized that there was no way she could go on like this permanently, no way she could live like this, *forever*. Mac had been right. Jewel had been right. Everything her heart had told her had been right. If only she hadn't waited so long to listen.

Here she was, right in the middle of her big moment, the kind of moment she only could have dreamed of a few weeks ago, and she was absolutely miserable.

When Evan finished speaking, Cassie applauded along with the crowd, wearing her ill-gotten dress and her false smile. She was ready to shed all of those things, but this still wasn't the moment to do it. So instead, she merely watched Evan, his eyes smiling toward her, as he left the podium and returned to his seat. Under the table, she took his hand and squeezed it very tightly. She thought of everything they'd shared and tried to savor it. Because she knew it would all be coming to a tragic end very soon.

CASSIE AND EVAN rode in his Saab down the dark, rain-slick streets of Chicago. Sometime after she'd spoken to Mac, the skies had opened, and it continued to drizzle still now. She hoped Mac had found some shelter from the storm.

Evan talked non-stop, his voice brimming with happiness. He spoke of his hopes for the future of Princess, his joy at attending the banquet with her on his arm, and how good it would be to get her home where they could be alone.

Cassie barely heard him, though. Instead, she sat in

silence, searching desperately for the words, the way to tell him the truth. It would happen tonight. Because it had to. She wasn't sure when or how—she only knew it was building inside her, tightening her chest, making it hard to breathe. Soon the truth would find its way out.

Evan seemed so completely content that he didn't even notice her quietness. He smiled over at her frequently, his expression that of a man who had it all.

"Have any mints?" he asked while they waited at a stoplight. "I want to freshen my breath up for you before we get home." He ended with a playful wink.

Cassie drew her purse up between them and began to dig inside. Finding a stick of peppermint gum, she held it out to him.

"What's this?" he asked.

"Gum," she said. "I don't have any mints."

"No," he said, "this." She looked down to see him reaching toward her purse, to the…*bright pink feather that protruded from it!* Oh God—it was from that horrible cat mask! She'd been in such a rush in between shopping and dinner that she'd forgotten to take it out of her purse!

"It's nothing," she said, brushing the feather away and then quickly zipping the purse shut, trapping the mask inside. Admitting she was the weird yellow-gloved, big-lipped catwoman who had waited on him was *not* the way to tell Evan the truth.

A few minutes later, he glided the car smoothly into a parking spot near his condo. He'd let the feather question go, but her heart still pumped wildly from the incident. The rain had picked up again and created a veil around the car, leaving Cassie to feel shut in and wishing for some route of escape.

When she reached for the door handle, Evan said, "Wait."

"What? Why?"

His voice softened. "Because it's pouring and I don't want you to ruin your dress. And because you look so beautiful. And because I don't want this night to end."

Oh no. As she glanced into those green eyes that had the power to hold her captive, she realized he had that romantic look about him—a look she normally adored, but she just couldn't deal with it right now.

It was too late, though, and protests were useless. Evan's hand was on her knee, his mouth pressing sensually against hers as his tongue edging its way between her lips. And she kissed him back. Because she couldn't help it. She parted her lips and let his tongue slip inside to gently circle hers.

"Do you have any idea how much you've changed my life?" he breathed in her ear. "You've made me realize that it's not all about business and money, that you have to make time for the important things. And *you*, honey, have become a very important part of my life. I love you."

Cassandra stopped kissing him then, the mounting guilt pouring over her as freely as the rain that blanketed the streets outside.

And she felt something break inside her. Something big.

And then she started to cry.

Evan pulled back from her slightly. "What is it, baby? What's wrong? What did I do?"

"It's not you," she said through her tears. "It's me."

"What do you mean, Cassandra?"

Oh God, he looked so confused. And she wanted to make up another lie, one that would explain her tears in some harmless way and put the moment behind them. She hesitated for a long, painful moment—but then, finally, she let the truth begin to leak free. "My name…isn't Cassandra. It's Cassie."

She wasn't looking at him now, but took in his perplexed expression even in her peripheral vision. "What?"

She could barely breathe, but she charged ahead anyway. "I'm not who you think I am, Evan. I'm a fake, and I'm a liar. I haven't been to Harvard, or any other college, and I'm not from Atlanta, I'm from Kentucky. I'm just a poor waitress trying to survive in the city and I'm so, so sorry I lied, but once it started…"

Cassie knew there was no good explanation. No wonder she'd never been able to find the words. There *were* none.

Unable to face his reaction to her horrible admission, Cassie then did the only thing she could think of. She opened the car door, grabbed her purse, and dashed away from Evan into the rain-filled night.

Chapter Fourteen

———❧———

EVAN SAT IN his car, dumbfounded. Had Cassandra really just said all those things and then run from his car out into the rain?

But then he remembered—she'd said her name *wasn't* Cassandra. What did that even mean? She didn't go to Harvard? She didn't come from Atlanta? What the hell had just happened here?

He released a sigh and tried to peer out into the rain that fell in sheets over the car, but he couldn't see a damn thing outside—it was as if she'd vanished into thin air.

Drawing his gaze back inside the car, his eyes fell on the strange pink feather on the floor of his car. He bent down and plucked it up. It was the only thing she'd left behind, the only thing he had to prove to himself that she'd really been here and that this had really just happened.

He twirled the feather between his fingers, thinking that it didn't seem altogether unfamiliar, but he didn't know why. He stared out into the rain-soaked night once again, this time simply trying to dissect and make sense of the things she'd said.

I'm just a poor waitress trying to survive in the city.

A waitress? Trying to survive? Did surviving include lying? Did surviving mean clawing her way to the top of the corporate ladder no matter what it took? Even if it required romping through a bed or two?

Evan shivered. It was hard to think of his Cassandra like that. She'd been a virgin, after all. *Hadn't* she? Hell, he barely knew what end was up at the moment—how could he be expected to remember if indeed he'd felt or seen any physical evidence of virginity? He'd never had any reason to doubt her, and she'd certainly *seemed* virginal enough, but what if all that was just a well-practiced act? Thinking back on her words a few minutes ago, it seemed more and more like she'd admitted that she'd just used him. For money? A nice place to live? A job? He wasn't sure. Maybe all of it.

His gaze came back to the pink feather still between his fingers. Where had he seen it before?

And then, like a bolt of lightning, it hit him. That silly waitress at the diner in the Mardi Gras mask. This feather had come from that mask. And Cassandra had said she was a *waitress*.

And then the further truth hit him like a ton of bricks.

The wide eyes, the pretty face, the silky hair—all the pieces fell into place in his mind. Cassandra was not only the waitress in the Mardi Gras mask—she was also the same waitress who'd spilled the iced tea on him!

It all began to make sense now. Sort of.

The waitress had been so nervous, and so sweet. Just like Cassandra. And so cute—also just like Cassandra. Evan couldn't believe he hadn't figured any of this out sooner. But then, he'd had no reason not to believe everything she'd said.

Still, he felt like an idiot. He'd fallen in love with her, after all. Completely and totally. No wonder he couldn't run his company—he couldn't even run his own life. That pretty girl had just marched into it and totally wrecked it without him even noticing.

If you're honest with yourself, weren't there moments...moments when she seemed too nervous? Moments when she didn't explain herself well? Moments you just let go because you were head over heels and didn't want anything to ever change that?

Shakespeare had been right—love *was* blind.

"Damn it," he said, banging his hand on the steering wheel. She'd made a fool of him. And she'd made a fool of Princess Cosmetics in the bargain.

And then—God—he remembered what it felt like to make love to her. How connected he'd felt to her—in bed and out. How he'd given his heart over to her completely.

But as the pain began rolling down over him in waves, and he worked to push it aside.

Why on earth had he thought he needed a woman to make him happy? And how could he have let himself be distracted from his job so easily? He sighed in disgust.

He'd be damned if *that* ever happened again.

Nonetheless, he stayed in the car for a very long time.

He didn't want to go in to the bed he'd shared with her this past week.

He didn't want to realize how alone he suddenly felt without her.

CASSIE WOKE UP on her hard mattress, sniffling, her pillow soaked with tears. Had she actually managed to cry in her sleep, too? Or maybe she'd never really slept at all...

She glanced helplessly at the black dress she'd dropped to the floor like a rag late last night. She didn't know if the once-lovely frock could be salvaged. Running for ten blocks in the rain before she could find a bus hadn't done the dress any favors. But then—what did it really matter? There'd be no place to wear something like that now anyway.

She could barely even recall what she'd said to Evan in his car last night. She only knew that a dam had broken inside her and let all her guilt flow free, out of her mouth and into the open. All she remembered clearly was the strange confusion in his eyes as he'd tried to piece together what she was saying. As she'd watched his expression twist and change, she'd felt the compulsion to vacate the car before his emotions grew into anger. She'd never seen those captivating green eyes turn furious before, and she hadn't wanted to. She hadn't wanted her last memory of him to be an angry one.

Wiping fresh tears from her sore eyes, she dragged herself out of bed. Though she barely knew why—she had nowhere to go and nothing to do. She'd never felt lonelier.

As she moped through her apartment, the place felt much emptier and more dank than it ever had before. She dug in a kitchen cabinet until she found the last of the ancient Pop Tarts that had sustained her the day after she'd twisted her ankle and took them to the couch. They were even staler than before, if that was possible.

But they at least filled her growling stomach. Which made her think of Mac. Of course, now he wouldn't get the job Evan had promised last night—a thought that made her heart break all over again, only in a different way this time.

There was something she *could* do for Mac, though. She could get herself up and dressed and do what she'd promised, what had given her bland life some meaning before Evan had come along. She could go to the shelter.

In one way, being around people was really the last thing Cassie wanted to do, but if she went to the Sunshine House today and then went to Eddie's to work all night, it might at least give her something to think about besides all she'd lost.

Who wanted to spend all day in a big, lonely, desolate warehouse anyway? She'd quickly grown used to being with Evan, feeling protected and cared for, and she already missed that companionship more than she could understand. She knew she deserved each and every ounce of depression weighing her down now, but she didn't have to lie there and wallow in it. No, she could wallow in it elsewhere and do something useful at the same time.

EVAN HAD SLEPT on the couch. And he'd dreamed of Cassandra—of her pretty smile and her innocent eyes. He woke in the morning feeling hurt, stupid, and betrayed. A night's rest had done nothing to dull his pain.

He lay on the leather sofa, one hand behind his head, staring blankly at the ceiling—but in his mind he saw her body and his, connected. Visions of their sex were simply too strong to push away. He thought of how incredible it felt to be inside her and to make her feel good. At least she hadn't faked *that*. Or at least he felt reasonably sure she hadn't.

For the first time, he began to wonder why she'd lied to him in the first place on the night of the charity benefit. They'd had fun and shared some wonderful kisses, and he'd practically fallen in love with her at first sight—so why had she found it necessary to paint herself as something she wasn't?

Was it really as he'd suspected last night—an attempt to sink her claws into his money by seeming more like him? Or was it something else?

Then Evan thought back to the iced tea incident and how embarrassed she'd been. She'd fallen all over herself trying to fix what she'd done—and she'd even bought him a tie to replace the one she ruined.

So it had probably come as a surprise to her to see him that night, and probably as an even bigger one that he'd asked her to dance. Was it possible she'd been so embarrassed that she simply didn't want him to figure out it was her?

He supposed that a guy who ran his own company could seem intimidating until you got to know him. Maybe she thought a guy like him wouldn't go for a girl like her without a few embellishments. And looking back on the iced tea incident, it was hard to imagine her as a person who would cook up a grand scheme to seduce him and steal his money.

Still, lies told from nervousness were one thing. But letting them continue, long-term, was another.

The hell of it was that he still wanted her. Even now, thinking about her in his old college T-shirt or in her sexy black suit at the office, he wanted her madly. Nothing that had happened last night had diminished how he felt for her. And it wasn't just sex. His heart hurt so much that he knew he was just as in love with her now as he had been yesterday.

What did a man do about such a predicament? He was a smart guy—he ran a major corporation, after all—so he should be able to figure this out. But planning corporate mergers was easier than this. His heart wasn't wrapped up nearly so tightly in Princess Cosmetics as it was in Cassandra.

Or was that Cassie?

Evan sighed and closed his eyes. It was Saturday and he didn't intend to move from his spot on the couch for a very long time. He planned on lying there doing nothing, sleeping some more if he felt like it. And the last thing he was going to do, he vowed to himself, was to think about *her* anymore.

It was all too confusing. And too fruitless.

He rolled over on the couch in disgust—with her, with himself, with the whole ugly situation. If only it were that easy.

CASSIE SERVED BOTH lunch and dinner at the Sunshine House. Although no one there could have thought her very sunshiny. She barely spoke, moving through the motions zombie-like.

"Cassie, are you all right today?" Ann had asked shortly after the first meal.

"Fine," Cassie had replied. Although she knew her eyes betrayed her. Enough, in fact, that Ann had apparently realized she shouldn't ask again.

Leaving the shelter around nine o'clock, she wandered out into the rain that had hung over Chicago for the past twenty-four hours. After catching a bus, she treated herself to a movie that she didn't really want to see. After all, why not spend a little more money that she didn't have? She was on a roll lately with that.

Who knew where the rent money would come from

this month? Maybe she'd undergo the humiliation of returning her suit to Irma at Marshall Fields if she could dig up the courage. Or maybe not. At the moment, she didn't really care.

She started up at the bright movie screen in a fairly empty theater, feeling lost. *This is bad, really bad. This is how people end up homeless—spending their money without a care toward tomorrow.* But she didn't want to go home, and she really had no place she *could* go until it was time to clean Eddie's at midnight.

She wandered into the diner at five 'til twelve, feeling soggy from so much rain. The place was empty save for Eddie, who sat counting down the cash drawer in the break room.

"Cassie," he said when he looked up to find her in the doorway. "How're you doing, kiddo?"

She couldn't help still being a little dumbfounded by this new, kinder, gentler Eddie. "Fine," she lied once more, settling into one of the plastic chairs across the table from him.

To her surprise, he reached out to pat her hand. "How's your family doing?"

Then she remembered. Her fictional aunt had died. It made her stomach hurt to be reminded. "Okay," she lied again. Then she changed the subject. "I hear you're headed to Florida."

"Yeah," he said, "I want to be closer to my folks. They're getting up there in years—and after you got me to thinking about my aunt, I realized how much we take people for granted, then miss them when they're gone. I don't want to do that with my mom and dad."

Cassie felt a little overwhelmed by his words, and stayed silent as Eddie shoved the money he'd counted into a vinyl pouch and rose to grab his jacket from a hook on the wall.

"Thanks for offering to do this tonight, Cass. I appreciate it."

"No problem, Eddie." Then, without knowing why, Cassie found herself rising from the table and giving Eddie a small hug. "Take care," she said.

He smiled down at her. "I'll see you on Monday. I won't be going for a few weeks yet."

"I think you're doing the right thing," she told him.

And she did. Family *was* important, and apparently something she'd said had opened Eddie's eyes to that. Could it be that one of her lies had actually done some good?

"You keep those blinds drawn tight," he said of the plate glass windows that fronted the building. "No need to call attention to you being here by yourself. Got it?"

"Got it."

Cassie watched Eddie depart into the rainy night, locking the glass door behind him.

Alone in the restaurant, she released a huge sigh at the task before her. It was a big job and not an ounce of it would be fun.

As she stuck her purse beneath the counter where the waitresses always stowed them, ready to get to work, she remembered. The mask. That horrible, stupid, ridiculous mask. So she retrieved her purse that quickly, opened it up, yanked the dumb thing out, and tossed it in the small trashcan nearby.

Next, she filled a bucket with hot, soapy water and decided to start by cleaning out the back of the counter. Besides purses, it also held menus, napkins, and myriad other things that didn't quite have a proper place, but she couldn't think of a time it had been given a good scrubbing since she'd started working at Eddie's. Unloading the shelves and setting the contents atop the counter, she gave the emptied space a thorough washing with soapy water and a sponge.

Rising to get herself a soft drink, she caught sight of the pink cat mask in the garbage. The sight made her stop and shake her head at how ridiculous she'd acted over the past two weeks. It was hard to believe the things love could do to a person. Then she got her drink and got back to work.

Next came scrubbing the floor around the stools and the counter. The waitresses usually mopped this area, but since Cassie wanted to do an extra-good job for Eddie, she felt that, just this once, it would be a task best done on hands and knees. She cleared the floor area around the counter and built-in stools, placing the nearly full wastebasket atop the table in a nearby booth. She had all night, and still wasn't particularly eager to go home—so why rush through this?

Look at me. Tattered blue jeans, water-pruned hands,

and a back that's beginning to ache. If Evan could only see her now. Cassie sighed, down on the floor scrubbing, thinking that this was how Cinderella's story was supposed to begin, not end. So much for fairy tales. And so much for fate.

When a knock came on the glass door, she nearly jumped out of her skin, her heartbeat kicking up. Was it a burglar? No, they didn't usually knock. Maybe Jewel? No, she had plans with Malcolm. *Must be Eddie. He must've forgotten something.*

Shee lifted her eyes to the rain-spattered door to find...

Evan.

On her knees, sponge in hand, she gasped. Then blinked. Was it really him? She blinked again, twice, then looked toward the glass door very hard. Oh God, it really was Evan—standing outside in the rain.

How had he found her? She'd confessed nothing about Fast Eddie's Diner, after all. And what on earth did he want?

Probably to yell at her. For masquerading as a Harvard graduate. For wasting his time. For everything that had taken place between them, from beginning to end.

Wasn't it enough that she was suffering? Wasn't the simple fact that she was working her fingers to the bone in the middle of the night an appropriate penance for her ridiculous Cinderella scheme?

"Let me in, Cassandra—I mean Cassie!" His voice came loud enough to cut through the rain and the glass that separated them, and she pulled in her breath upon realizing he'd called her by her real name.

"No!" she yelled back.

"Cassie, let me in! I love you!"

Okay, wait. She knew she couldn't have heard that last part correctly—his voice was muffled through the glass, after all.

But then he said it again. "I love you! And it was very sweet of you to send me that tie!"

Cassie gasped. That meant he hadn't just stumbled upon her here tonight through some weird kind of dumb luck. He knew. He remembered her. How humiliating.

But in the same instant, her heart flooded with joy. He'd just said he loved her!

She called to him from her spot on the floor near the counter. "You do?"

And she saw him nod through the raindrops dotting the glass. "Now will you let me in? I'm getting soaked out here."

Cassie rose hurriedly from beside the bucket and rushed to the door. Twisting the lock to let him come in from the rain, she felt as nervous and confused as she had the first time she'd laid on him two weeks before. Only now she felt stupid and guilty on top of it.

She locked the door behind him, then turned to where he stood near the booth where they'd first met, dripping and gorgeous. She didn't know what to say, but finally settled on, "How did you find me?"

"You weren't at home," he said, "but..." His expression went softer as he pulled a pink feather from his pocket. Then he happened to glance into the wastebasket on the table next to him and reached inside to pull out the cat mask. Studying it, he found the empty spot where the feather had once resided and held it in place. "It fits," he said. "So it has to be you."

Being reminded of the mask did nothing to help curb Cassie's guilt and humiliation. "Okay," she said, "so you found me. But...but..."

"But what?"

"But I lied to you," she told him. "About everything. Shouldn't you be hating me? Or calling me a gold digger?"

"*Are* you one?"

"No."

"I didn't think so," he said, shaking his head. "I tried to convince myself that you were, but I couldn't do it. You don't fit the mold. And I don't hate you, Cassie. I *can't* hate you—because I love you. And after thinking about this long and hard, I've come to the conclusion that if you found it necessary to tell me all those lies that you must have had a good reason."

"I *did have* a good reason," she explained. "Or, I mean, it seemed like a good reason at the time." She swallowed, lowered her gaze. "Actually, I suppose it was a lousy reason. But I just couldn't think straight when you were dancing with me and pulling me close and making me feel so incredible and special, and so much like I'd never felt before."

"Whatever it is, you can tell me," he said, his green eyes shining on her.

So she spoke from the heart. "Evan, that first day here when I spilled the tea on you, I was mortified. Then when you asked me to dance after dinner that night and I realized you didn't remember me, I couldn't bear to tell you I was the clumsy waitress who had ruined your tie. I wanted to be...someone you would want, someone from your world. I was so crazy about you that I couldn't think logically, and...well, I didn't think you'd find me too appealing like this," she said, looking down at herself, "the way I really am."

"That's where you're wrong," he whispered.

She blinked. "I am?"

"I love everything about you, honey, from the way you spilled iced tea on me to the way you started trying to help me fix my company to the way you make love to me with every ounce of yourself."

A veil of warmth crept up her face. "You can't really have loved the way I spilled iced tea on you."

He gave her a conceding grin. "Okay, I didn't. But I loved the way you blushed afterward."

"Really?"

"And I love the way you're blushing now. And the way your eyes get so big and round when you're a little surprised, a little flattered, the way you are right now."

Cassie sighed, bit her lip.

"And I really don't care where you grew up or what diplomas hang on your wall. All I really care about is being with you."

Cassie swallowed. This seemed too good to be true. "Oh, Evan," she said, a tear rolling down her cheek, "I didn't think you'd ever want to have anything to do with me again. Especially after I let the lie go on and on. But lying was so dumb in the first place that I couldn't bear to admit it to you. Does that make any sense?" She held her hands out helplessly.

"I let a lie exist between us, too. Remember?"

"Yes," she said, "but your lie…your lie…well, it was nothing compared to this."

"A lie is a lie, Cassie. And you forgave me the moment I told you the truth."

"So," she began uncertainly, "does that mean…that you can actually find it in your heart…to forgive me? For all of this?"

He smiled down at her. "How about if I chalk it up to bad judgment?"

She nodded. "I would like that."

"You know," he said, growing suddenly serious, "I wasn't going to do this. I wasn't going to come searching for you or making up with you. I was going to convince myself that I didn't need you in my life and that love wasn't worth hurting over." Then he took *her* wet hands into *his* wet hands. "But I couldn't do it because it wasn't true. And because I thought there'd been enough untruths in our relationship already. And because the only truth I can see—the truth I keep coming back to over and over again—is that I love you, Cassie, and I want to spend my life with you."

Her legs began to crumble beneath her, but Evan held her up. "You what?"

"I want to marry you," he told her. Then he lowered his knee to the wet linoleum. "Will you marry me, Cassie? Will you be my wife?"

Cassie's eyes flew open wide. "I do and I will," she said breathlessly. "And I promise, I'm not lying this time."

Cassie blinked then, to make sure she wasn't dreaming. But in the second she opened them, Evan brought his mouth down on hers in a slow, sensual kiss that rocked her senses and reminded how wonderful he could make her feel.

"This is real," she murmured.

"And it's forever," he whispered against her lips.

Look for more classic Toni Blake reissues, including:

The Guy Next Door
The Bewitching Hour

And don't miss any of these contemporary romance titles
from Toni Blake:

The Coral Cove Series:
All I Want Is You
Love Me If You Dare
Take Me All The Way

The Destiny Series:
One Reckless Summer
Sugar Creek
Whisper Falls
Holly Lane
Willow Springs
Half Moon Hill

Other Titles:
Wildest Dreams
The Red Diary
Letters to a Secret Lover
Tempt Me Tonight
Swept Away

About the Author

Toni Blake's love of writing began when she won an essay contest in the fifth grade. Soon after, she penned her first novel, nineteen notebook pages long. Since then, Toni has become a RITA™-nominated author of more than twenty contemporary romance novels, her books have received the National Readers Choice Award and Bookseller's Best Award, and her work has been excerpted in *Cosmo*. Toni lives in the Midwest and enjoys traveling, crafts, and spending time outdoors. Learn more about Toni and her books at www.toniblake.com, or sign up for her newsletter and follow her on Facebook to get all the latest news and have a chance to win signed books and other prizes.

CPSIA information can be obtained at www.ICGtesting.com
Printed in the USA
LVOW08s1707250716

497699LV00007B/620/P